Daniel Locke
and the Tower of Eden

Marty Longson

ISBN   978-1468006407

Dedicated to Trish, Rylie, Keira, Dianne, and Larry.

-There is magic in the world, sometimes you just have to work hard to find it.

PROGLOGUE – DOWN IN A HOLE

The black and chrome Bugatti Veyron flew around the corner and blasted around the hillside. The powerful engine roared as the car accelerated through a straight section of road and braked hard for the coming switch back corner. The trees blurred by and mountain air whistled through the car's open windows. Daniel Locke sat behind the wheel humming quietly as the car drifted around a long sweeping curve. The wind ruffled his short brown hair and threatened to tear the sunglasses from his face as he sped along his own private road. He drove the car like an artist, flinging it skillfully through the apex of each corner and accelerating through the straightaways. As he drove, the roadside to his right gave away to a gentle treed slope leading up to a majestic sight. At the top of the hill was a modern day castle.

The impressive stonework of the castle towered over the sprawling valley below. The flowing rooflines and tall stone towers were majestic but simple. Large stained glass windows fronted the main building and stone balconies dotted the walls here and there. The ancient looking castle was also a modern marvel of technology. It had sealed LED stained glass windows that were capable of changing colors at a whim and a thermal heating and cooling system that ran deep into the earth. The castle even had its own state of the art hydroelectric plant. Large tubular wave catchers lay submerged just off the coast. The wave catchers captured the crushing power of the pacific oceans surf as it battered the Californian coastline.

The Bugatti slid to a stop at the crest of the hill as the castle grounds came into sight again. The tall peaks and towers stood silhouetted in the fading light of the setting sun. He paused a moment to take in the beautiful scenery. Daniel breathed in deeply, smelling and tasting the bite of fresh salty ocean air.

This was all for his family. This was a way to bring them all closer. The last few years had been hard on his family. His wife, Jolie, was diagnosed with cancer just over a year ago and his son Daniel junior was getting ready to tour Europe after his boarding school graduation ceremonies next week. Daniel was still trying to convince his son to spend his year off at home instead of abroad.

Daniel Locke looked back down the slope of the hill, to the road that snaked down into the valley. The road was calling him again. His pulse started to race and his breathing quickened in anticipation. He looked back to the castle with the ocean backing it, as the sun burned low over the horizon. With a quick turn of the steering wheel and a blip of the throttle, the Veyron's rear-end whipped around 180 degrees. He was just about to start the valley descent again when his cell phone rang. He touched the Bluetooth button to answer.

"Hello?" Daniel said.

"Daniel Thomas Locke you better not be turning that toy of yours around again for another run."

It was his wife, Jolie.

"No love I," he began to say.

"You have people waiting for you in the grand room. You can't ignore them again Daniel," she said, her tone smooth and strong.

"Yes love," he began again. His wife had a knack for interrupting.

"Oh, before I forget, Hank called up from the orchard. He said something about his tractor acting funny. He wanted you to stop by before it gets too dark."

"Thank you Jolie. I'll be right up," he looked down the hillside again, at the thick forest below and the orchard off in the distance. He felt a slight tugging sensation in his chest. Hank was a good friend and his closest neighbour, actually his only neighbour in the whole valley. If the old man had asked for help, it was probably for a good reason.

"Actually on second thought," he told Jolie. "Have a couple bottles of wine sent up to the geek squad in the grand room and let them know I'll be right up after I help Hank."

"Daniel..." she said, but her tone was soft and breathy.

He laughed at his wife and smiled wide.

"See ya soon love," he said and clicked off the phone.

The team of engineers and scientists he had working on the hydro plant could wait a little while longer. After all, old Hank needed his help.

The Veyron's engine revved and the tires smoked as the car launched itself down the hill.

The orchard came into view after several minutes of hard driving and Daniel slowed the car down to a crawl. The ancient orchard occupied a massive piece of property with apple trees spreading out as far as the eye could see. The forest of trees covered acres of land along this stretch of valley floor. Hank had once told him this piece of land had been in

3

his family for generations. Hank's farmhouse and apple store came into view as Daniel turned into the parking lot.

Daniel stretched as he got out of the car and looked around for his friend. The farmhouse and store were both dark and quiet.

"Hank? Where are you old man?" he called out into the twilight.

Daniel was just walking around the edge of the orchard when he spotted the tractor. The little red tractor had its back tires sunk deep into a soft patch of earth.

"Hank I got your message," he said a little louder. "You need help with that tractor?" he called into the woods.

Silence. The orchard was quiet and nothing moved in the fading light.

"Maybe old Hank had gone back to his work shed for some tools," Daniel said muttering to himself.

Daniel walked over to the sunken tractor. Both rear wheels were stuck deep in the earth. He looked under the front tires and pressed down hard on the ground near them. The ground seemed solid enough, and the mud around the rear wheels really wasn't that deep. Maybe Hank just gave up too easily.

He hopped up on the tractor and found the keys still in the ignition. Daniel was just reaching for the starter when the ground shuddered and gave away beneath him and the tractor.

When the dust finally cleared, he was still sitting on the tractor. The muddy hole however, was about thirty feet above his head. Stunned and a bit confused, he looked around at where the tractor had landed. It was a large round chamber with a dark smooth surface of stone. The light from above barely lit the area around the tractor.

Daniel flicked on the ignition switch and then toggled the headlights. The room around him flooded with blazing light. It was some sort of an underground storage room. Objects were carefully stored on racks, shelves, or tables around the outside of the circular room. Daniel looked for an exit to the room but quickly realized he was out of luck. The walls around him appeared to be one thick solid mass, smooth and unbroken except for the hole, high above.

"This must be an old farm cellar," he said as he slid from the tractor and patted around his pockets for his cell phone. "Damn it," he cursed loudly realizing the phone was sitting back in his car.

He would have to wait for Hank to make his way back to the tractor or for his wife to send someone out looking for him. Since he had the time, he decided to look around the room a little closer. Several dusty objects glittered softly in the harsh headlights of the tractor. His curiosity only grew as he wandered around the large room. There was a lot of dirt and dust down here but wherever he was, it wasn't a farmer's cellar.

Dirt had layered itself over everything in the room. He walked over to the nearest table and brushed away an inch of rich fertile soil off the top. What he uncovered was something smooth and hard. Delicately he brushed more dirt off it and then pulled a long rod from its earthen tomb. It was a clear crystal stick about two feet long.

He tapped one end of the stick on the table to shake off some of the remaining dirt. As the stick came down for a second little tap, thunder filled his ears and blue lightning danced in his eyes.

EDEN 1 – ENTER THE DRAGON

The shiny black Ducati motorcycle pulled off the main road and into the diner's gravel parking lot. There was an open spot just under the Flo's Diner sign, so he pulled in and slid off the bike. The rider was a lean young man with short brown hair and sharp green eyes. He wore a black riding jacket and jeans. A black and grey helmet had its visor open to the summer breeze. The young man's bright green eyes scanned the lot and the small town around him. A helicopter buzzed by overhead as a convoy of large green trucks rumbled down the quiet street in front of the diner. Opening his jacket, the young man reached for his cell phone. He re-read an email message he had gotten earlier that morning.

From: James
To: Indy

The flooding around Appleton hasn't subsided yet but the weather looks like it has cleared up. If you still insist on riding your bike all the way here, I may have found someone to help. One of my contacts in town is a young waitress named Joslyn McCloud. Look for her at Flo's Diner when you arrive, she should be on the day shift.

P.S. I hope you're enjoying your graduation present.

After putting his cell phone back into his jacket pocket, he headed for the diner. The young man tucked his helmet under his arm and walked through the glass doors and into the diner.

Inside, the diner's lunchtime crowd was packed into booths and tables. Their chatter filled the air as he made his way through the room. Indy saw an open barstool at the counter and headed over to it. He sat down on the stool, resting his helmet under one elbow.

He scanned the crowd around him looking for his contact. Most of the patrons were busy watching a news broadcast on the diners overhead TVs. Just then a pretty blonde waitress walked by carrying a full platter of food. The girl looked about his age, around sixteen or seventeen. She was good looking with long curly hair and a bright infectious grin. The waitress gave him a quick wink as she passed but kept moving through the diner. A glance at her nametag told him it was Joslyn.

A large aproned bartender passed by in her wake, heading towards a large TV mounted in the corner of the room. His large meaty hand reached up to the TV and turned up the volume. The buzz around the room quieted as more heads swivelled to watch the TV.

"Breaking news... This just in from Appleton, California..."

"U.S. officials have declared a state of emergency in this small community in northern California. Their problems started last Friday night during a freak electrical storm when several of the town's electrical substations overloaded. To add to their troubles the people there have also been dealing with heavy rains and flooding over the last week. The National

Guard is on hand, aiding efforts to help reinforce the town and nearby river with sand bags. The area is still…"

His view of the TV was blocked by a sturdy grey haired waitress. She had stepped in front of him and was smiling down at him. "Hey there handsome, what can I getcha," she asked.

Indy smiled up at her and pointed to a neighbour's piece of apple pie on the counter beside him.

"Can I get a slice of pie?" he asked.

"Sure thing hon, be right back." The waitress smiled at him warmly and spun away to get his pie.

While his waitress was off getting the apple pie, Indy looked around the small diner for Joslyn. He spotted her quickly and when he was finally able to make eye contact, he waved her over. When she came over, he smiled and noted her nametag again.

"Joslyn?" he asked.

The blonde nodded her head once and waited. Looking him up and down.

"My name is Indy," he said with a lopsided grin and stretched out his hand. "I was told by a friend you were the one to talk to if I wanted to get up to the castle. I want to get up there today, if I could."

She took his offered hand and shook it firmly. "Sure I can get you up there. My dad is overseeing the helicopters coming in and going out. It will cost ya though," Joslyn said with a smile.

"Oh," she laughed. "No, that came out wrong," Joslyn blushed as she corrected herself. "Things have been a little weird around here the last couple of days and I just want some answers. When you get up to the castle, you just let me know what's what."

She looked around the diner and then back at him. Their eyes connected for an instant before he looked away, his heart skipping a beat.

"So what do you want to know?" he had to swallow a lump in his throat as he asked.

Joslyn looked him in the eyes, maybe trying to gauge his knowledge of the castle and its situation.

"Well my mom told me a couple guys from the castle were all over town yesterday. They wanted to know if anyone had any antique crystal they wanted to sell. Mom said they were offering big money too. She said they told her something about the crystals being an anniversary gift for Mrs. Locke."

Indy nodded knowingly and smiled.

Joslyn leaned a little closer to him. Her hair smelled like strawberries. "I heard that billionaire built the castle for his wife as a retirement gift. That's so romantic," she gushed. "I would just love to get a peek at the inside. My dad took us up there a few weeks ago, but we didn't even get a chance to go in. We had to wait outside by a massive fountain."

As she pulled back from his ear, she ran a finger over his shoulder. She noticed the black crystal dragon pendant dangling from a gold necklace around his neck.

"Oh that's pretty," she said.

Indy put a hand to it. "Thanks... It was my grandfathers," he said slowly.

Indy thought back to the night a few days ago. He had been packing a few of his grandparent's things for his father when he had come across the dragon crystal. Some of the other antique crystals he had found there were packed away

9

inside his bike packs. The necklace was something he had found amongst their things that he wanted to keep for himself. The dragon pendant seemed to call to him as he gazed upon it. It was a powerful looking beast and it had drawn his eye instantly.

He had been going through his parent's old dusty attic at the time. The dragon was unique among the odd collection of assorted crystal ducks and Christmas bulbs scattered around the attic. The dragon was also the only crystal in the bunch that was midnight black.

"I haven't seen the castle yet but I am on the way up there now," Indy said. "But since the floods have closed all roads leading to the castle, I need another way up there."

The older waitress came by just then. She smiled at Joslyn and put the pie down in front of Indy.

"Joslyn, don't talk this man's ear off," she said with a honeyed tone. "You've got customers waiting."

Joslyn nodded at the other waitress and the heavy woman moved off to see to other customers.

Joslyn turned back his way and said, "Some of the workers came in here last night. They said that lately the castle was as busy as a beehive. People were running all over the place and there was a constant stream of helicopters flying in and out. They have a helipad set up here, just outside of town. I could get you a seat on the next chopper out if you want, Indy."

Indy shook his head with an emphatic no. "Thanks but I'll stick with my bike. I really don't like flying if I can help it. Got any other ideas?"

"Is that your bike out there, the Ducati?" she asked but continued without waiting for an answer. "Well I know an old hunting trail. I think it hooks up to the main road somewhere after the flood plains. The trail is pretty smooth, so I think you should be able to make it without too much trouble."

Indy smiled again and said, "That would be excellent."

"I could show you, if you've got room on that bike for me?" she offered.

"Sure you can tag along if you like," he said casually even as his heart threatened to burst through his ribs.

"Wendy?" Joslyn called out to the other waitress. "Mind if I leave a bit early today?"

The older grey haired woman called back. "Sure thing dear, just finish up with the Flemings. I can cover you until your sister shows up."

"Thanks Wendy!" Joslyn called. She patted Indy lightly on the shoulder. "Finish up that pie and I will meet you outside. I just need to change out of this uniform and grab a few things from the back."

Not long after that, they were riding across the ridge high above Appleton. Joslyn had changed from her waitress uniform and into a more casual outfit. Now she was in a loose t-shirt, jeans, and brown hiking boots. Following her directions, Indy took several trails through the woods above Appleton. The Ducati's tires were soaking up the off road abuse of a well-used hunting trail as they looked down over the valley below. They could see the whole valley spreading out below them from the high rocky ridge. The National Guard was working hard on retaining walls of sandbags and reinforcing dykes along the river in hopes to prevent further flooding. They also saw some large farm equipment and other heavy machinery working along the banks as they darted along the ridgeline path.

The hunter's trail they rode was well worn and well above the flood plain. Luckily, the dirt trail was fairly dry and it didn't take more than an hour or so to get through the woods and back to the main road. The Ducati's touring tires fared much better on the open paved road and Indy poured on the speed.

They could see the castle in the distance when all of a sudden, the bike coughed and shut down. It coasted to a stop as the two riders looked around.

"Indy, look at that!" Joslyn said. Joslyn was pointing to the road behind them. Indy looked back to see what she was pointing at.

Both sides of the road were thick with grass and small bushes around twenty feet behind them. Further back towards Appleton the roadside was well trimmed and clear of weeds. Even the air itself seemed to shimmer around the same area. At first, he had thought it was just light reflecting off his visor shield. When he flipped his helmet visor open, he realized it was something very different.

"Weird... It's almost like an aurora," Indy said. "Kind of like the northern lights in Canada."

Joslyn hopped off the back and Indy set the bike on its kickstand. He was just about to follow her back to the line of shimmering air, when it happened. Indy had just reached up to unzip his jacket when his hand brushed his necklace. His head swam as the world around him spun. Indy dropped to one knee as blue electricity flared around him. His mouth opened to yell for Joslyn, but nothing came out. He ripped off his jacket and looked at his bare arms. The dragon pendant around his neck burned brightly and began to pulse. Even

Indy's skin started to glow and pulse in time with the pendant. When the dragon finally stopped burning with the eerie blue light, his skin flashed black for an instant and then turned back to its normal healthy white.

Indy gasped for breath and put his hand to his throat. Something warm tingled at his throat just under his collar. His hand felt around his neck, the gold necklace was still there but the crystal dragon was gone.

"Indy?" Joslyn called to him. Joslyn ran to his side and helped him to his feet. "You ok," she asked.

"Yeah," he said. "Just a little dizzy… I guess I've been on the road to long, maybe I'm just tired."

He wasn't sure what just happened, maybe he had just imagined the blue light. He didn't want Joslyn to think he was a nut case so he just kept quiet, hoping it was just motion sickness or something. It upset him that the dragon crystal was missing though.

He accepted her help to steady himself and she bent down to pick up his jacket. Thankfully, there was no lingering dizziness as he stood back up, but his head throbbed with a dull headache.

"Thanks," he said as he slid his arms back into the jacket. Indy stepped over to his bike and tried the starter. The Ducati purred to life. "Hmmm, that was weird," Indy put the whole thing up to his inexperience on his new bike. Nevertheless, he promised himself to get the bike checked out as soon as he could.

They got back onto the bike after giving the shimmering aurora another curious glance. As he drove off his head was throbbing and all he could think of was getting to the castle for a little rest. The road ahead blurred beneath them as they headed towards the castle on the hillside.

The bike pulled up to the massive gates of the castle wall and they waited patiently as a guard came out of a small stone building attached to the wall. The man was in his fifties and dressed in a dark blue guard uniform, complete with radio and gun holster. Indy could see the black gun poking out of the holster on his hip. The guard was slightly overweight but as the man came closer to their motorcycle, they both had to look up to see him. He had to be over six foot five.

"Sorry kids you're going to have to come back later," the guard said gruffly. "We're not accepting visitors right now."

Joslyn spoke up, "I thought you guys were still looking for antique crystals?"

The guard shook his head. "Sorry Miss, we are not accepting anything at the moment. Mr. Locke has more than enough things to deal with at this time. If you want, you could leave your name and any packages with me. I will see he gets them."

"Look buddy," Joslyn started. "Why don't you get on your little walkie talkie there and tell someone with a little more authority then you, that Joslyn McCloud is out here."

The guards pale face stared blankly at her.

"Joslyn McCloud," she huffed. "You know... the sheriff's daughter."

Indy turned to look a little closer at the blonde girl sitting behind him and silently mouthed. "Sheriff?"

She blushed slightly but nodded yes, all the while keeping her gaze locked on the guard. "And my guest, Indy... Well I guess I never did get your last name did I," she giggled slightly embarrassed.

"Look Ms. McCloud," The guard said. "The Locke's are busy people they just-"

"Just call up to the house... Please," she begged. "Ask for James."

"Ok," The guard huffed. "I'll call it in. No promises though," The guard said as he started to turn away. He took two steps before turning back again.

He looked down at Indy and asked, "What was your name kid?"

Indy pulled his helmet off. "It's Daniel Locke, junior."

The guard did a quick double take as Indy set his helmet down on his gas tank.

"Daniel junior?" The guard asked, stuttering a little. "Sorry sir... I didn't recognize you. I mean you had your helmet on and..."

"No harm done, Mr.?" Indy said, waiting for the man's name.

"Lucas sir, Barney Lucas. I'll get that gate for you Mr. Locke. Do you want me to call ahead?" the guard asked politely.

Indy nodded and said, "Thank you Mr. Lucas."

Joslyn had a hurt look on her face as the guard went back into his office to open the gate.

"Daniel Locke junior," she asked and smacked him lightly on the shoulder. "You could have said something a little earlier."

Indy looked back slyly. "Ya, but where is the fun in that. By the way only my friends call me Indy."

"You could have told me you know," she pouted. "You didn't need my help getting in here."

Indy smiled at her as he slid his helmet back on.

15

"Ya, but then you wouldn't have gotten the chance to look around inside the castle," he turned to the gates as they started to open with a wide smile on his face.

The large iron bars of the gate motored open silently, then clanged loudly as they stopped against the wall. As they rode through the gates, the castle grounds rolled out before them, green leafed oak trees flanked both sides of the road as they headed towards the castle.

EDEN 2 – HOME FOR A REST

Inside the main gates, the road split off in several places as the castle's main doors came into view. The main house was set on the highest part of the ridge ahead of them with four corner towers and a fifth taller one at center. To the left of the main building there was a helipad complete with large fog lights. The cement pad had a giant letter H painted in white. There wasn't a helicopter on it now but there were several trucks and a large hanger nearby.

On the other side of the road, they passed a few smaller buildings before coming around a large fountain to the main doors. A large stained glass window looked down at them over top two large heavy wooden doors.

"Whoa," Joslyn said.

"Ya," Indy replied. "It looks like they went all out this time. My dad was referring to it as the rest home during its building phase. I guess he was planning on retiring sometime this year to spend a little more time with mom and me."

"This is amazing," Joslyn said with awe as she stared up at several stone gargoyles hanging from the walls.

Together they walked up to the massive carved wooden doors and as they did the door on the left opened.

"Indy!" A man stood before them with a solid jaw and wide shoulders. He wore a white button down shirt, a black vest that barely hid his solid build and a pair of dress pants. The man's dark eyes glanced over them with a brooding look. "You have kept your parents waiting," he said. His expression eased as his face broke into a wide grin. "But who is your beautiful friend?"

"James," Indy said. "This is Joslyn McCloud."

Joslyn put a hand forth to shake with James. "It's nice to finally meet you James."

James took her offered hand with a small bow.

"It's very nice to meet you as well, Joslyn," he said. "Your father has spoken very highly of you, but he failed to mention how beautiful you are. I will have to thank him for recommending such a capable guide for Indy."

Indy nodded at James and said, "James here is my father's jack of all trades. He is like a Swiss army knife in a three-piece suit. James has been with our family for years."

James bowed deeply to Indy and motioned them both inside.

"Please let me show you inside," he said. "Your parents are waiting in the great room. Allow me to show you the way."

They walked through castle's grand entrance hall. The floor was a dark smooth granite and the walls a deep rich wood. Crystal chandeliers graced the ceiling and the lighting fixtures on the wall were a dark metal grey. The grand hallway that towered over them took several turns before they came to a set of polished oak doors.

They could hear raised voices inside the room as James paused outside the twin doors.

"We can't possibly know the dangers," A gravelly voice was saying. "You must let me shut-"

"No. We can't do that," A strong firm voice said in reply. "We have an amazing opportunity here. Who knows what world changing technologies we could discover."

James cracked the door open silently and led the kids inside. He raised a single finger to his lips and urged their silence.

"Mr. Locke we need to be very careful. There are so many unknowns in this case. We have no idea of the consequences of this... Power." The gravelly voice belonged to an older man with short grey hair wearing a white lab coat. The old man looked like he hadn't slept in weeks. Dark black circles sagged under his eyes and wild grey hair topped his head. The man reminded Indy of a small frail grandfather. "Please reconsider," he said. "My science team has gathered several more of the artifacts and we have begun testing the effects-"

"No, no, no." Daniel Locke stood at the front of the room waving his hands around wildly. His father was a spitting image of Indy. Only the wrinkles around his eyes and a slightly receding hairline were different. "What I have found here is the single most important discovery this world has ever known. I will not withhold the knowledge of it from the world."

The man in the lab coat was shaking his head. "But the world in general will not harness these things for good," he said. "I fear someone will find a way to turn these artifacts to great evil."

"We can't let that happen. We have a chance to do something great, something that will make this world a better place," Indy's father said as he noticed the trio waiting at the far end of the room. "I say we must appeal to the international community. We must make sure that what we have found is used for the greater good."

"That is insane," The scientist was saying. "The U.S. military will just come in and brush us out of the way at the first whiff of any possible advanced technology. They will take over this whole valley and we'll be lucky if they don't make us just disappear in the process."

Indy's father stood and said, "Okay Doc. We will keep our findings from the world for the time being. However, I still see the need to continue to bring in more people. I can hire more people to search for these crystals and explore these newly found artifacts. However, I also will continue bringing in selected terminally ill patients. We have a duty to fulfill... we must do what little we can in any case. Imagine if we are able to save just one person in a thousand."

Daniel Locke started pacing the floor, deep in thought. He stopped pacing and looked hard at the old man.

"Doctor," he said with an air of command. "I want you to continue experimenting, but I want you to move your labs out of the main buildings and down to the hydro plant. Just to be safe. If you need anything at all, contact James."

"James!" Daniel called. "Make sure the doctor has what he needs. Make it a priority."

"Yes sir," James said stiffly and nodded at the man in the lab jacket.

Indy stepped out from behind his hulking butler and waved at his father.

"Dad!" he yelled.

"Junior," Daniel said in greeting. "It's about time you showed up. I could have used you here days ago. I have a lot to share with you. We couldn't risk any information leaks so I didn't want to tell you over the phone."

"Please excuse us… everyone out," he said to the others in the room. Out, out, out. I need some family time. James, please go get my wife and let her know junior is home."

James and the other man moved from the room and when the room quieted, Indy introduced Joslyn to his father.

"Dad," he said. "This is my friend Joslyn McCloud. Her father is sheriff McCloud from Appleton."

Daniel Locke strode down from the raised section of floor to grab his son in a fierce hug. "I have missed you junior."

"Dad…" Indy whined.

"Ah, and you Ms. McCloud, I assume it was you that helped my wayward son get through the flood lands."

"Yes sir Mr. Locke," she said.

"Please, please call me Dan or Daniel. I've heard it's quite a mess down there, eh? I have several teams working with the National Guard to help clear the roads and rebuild the dykes along the river."

"Daniel? Danny!" A soft female voice cried out.

Indy's mom had walked in through a rear door in the grand hall. She looked radiant, tall and…

"Mom?" Indy shouted. "Mom, where is your chair? Oh my god…You're walking!"

Mrs. Locke was moving slowly and with the aid of a tall white walking staff but she wasn't in her usual electric wheel chair. A chair she had been in for over a year now. A couple years ago, she had been in a car crash that had almost killed her. They had gotten even more bad news after the crash when x-rays revealed a cancerous growth on her brain. All the best doctors and medicine in the world couldn't completely fix her but his dad had tried. Numerous surgeries had followed and the radiation treatments had finally sent the cancer into remission. The whole ordeal had left her weak and forever tired. Now she was up and walking!

Indy ran to her for a hug but slowed when the staff she was holding seemed to catch the light and flared a brilliant blue.

"What is that?" Indy asked, coming up short.

His father walked up behind him. "That is the key to many questions junior," he said. "Right now we have many more questions than answers," he nodded at the staff. "All we really know is that the longer your mom holds that staff, the faster she has healed. It started happening within days after I found it. The doctor thinks that in a day or two more your mom will be completely healed."

Indy and Joslyn stood there with awed expressions on their face. Doubts clearly flickered across both of their faces. Curiosity finally won out for Indy.

"Where did you get it?" he asked. "What is it? How does it work?" More questions exploded in Indy's head as the rapid fire questions poured from his mouth.

"Is it magic?" Joslyn asked as the staff flared again with an eerie blue light.

"We don't know for sure," Jolie said softly. "Daniel has a few of the brightest minds we could find looking at it. They have scanned it with every manner of tool known to man. They haven't come back with much though and they can't explain how it works or even what powers it. Through trial and error, I have found that the healing it can do applies to every known malady. It cures everything from a paper cut to cancer. It's like it just regenerates any one and anything that it touches."

"It just takes time though," Jolie said with a brilliant smile. "It's not an instant fix. But you can feel it working," her brown eyes closed for an instant as the blue light flared again. "It's like ice running through your veins but it's so energizing. Let me show you. It might be easier to explain if you feel it for yourself," she lifted the end of the staff and lowered it to her sons shoulder.

He felt nothing. His head still ached and his feet were still tired. The glow of the staff faded as well, as it rested on his shoulder.

His mom didn't notice the quizzical look on his face as she lifted the staff away from his shoulder.

"Joslyn," she asked. "Would you like to try it too?"

Joslyn's eyes went wide and she nodded slowly. The staff swung over to her shoulder and reignited blue as it came to rest there. The light pulsed several times and a hum filled the room.

Joslyn's eyes closed and she gasped. "It's incredible!" she said in complete awe.

Jolie returned the staff to the floor and drew in a deep breath as she relaxed. "We started converting rooms as soon as we realized what we had. We asked a few people we knew if they had any family in need. Daniel began to fly in anyone we could find that was willing to try an extremely experimental healing technique. People have already been flown in and in every single case so far the healing has started to work."

"We started with the people that were in the most desperate need of healing," Jolie said as she walked over to her husband and wrapped her one free arm around his shoulder. "He's got me running around healing these people all day. I bet it would be all night too if he had his way."

"Are all these people staying in the castle?" Indy asked.

Jolie's long brown hair fell in her eyes as she nodded. "Until we have a retreat style spa finished we have converted one of the castle's guest wings into a hospital wing."

"What about the patients," Joslyn said. "What are you telling them? You cannot seriously be telling these people you can heal them with a magic stick. People would think you're a bunch of nuts up here if that ever got out."

"Actually we have a way around telling them. It was something that James thought up," Daniel said. "He suggested we have papers drawn up that basically say that if they agree to become part of an experimental medical group then they are not allowed to disclose our procedures to anyone."

"Once they have agreed to our terms, we get them set up with a hospital bed and an IV saline solution. Jolie comes around once a day after the patients are treated a dose of Valium. None of the patients ever see the staff."

A siren blipped several times in the distance.

"I have to go," Daniel said. "That siren means another patient is being airlifted in. Why don't you two go explore the grounds? His father nodded and grinned at his son as he reached for his wife's elbow. "Go see James before you go," he said, "He will get you setup and give you a tour of the castle.

"Nice meeting you Joslyn, James told me how helpful you have been," Jolie said. "You're welcome to stay and visit as long as you like. The chopper can give you a lift back to town anytime you wish to head back."

Daniel stepped closer to Joslyn and looked her straight in the eye. "Joslyn," he said. "It's really important that you don't mention this staff to anyone just yet. We have been considering setting up an international news conference to tell the world, but we are still working out the details. I wouldn't want anything slipping out before its time."

Joslyn nodded in agreement.

Daniel nodded at them in return and swept from the room with his wife on his arm.

EDEN 3 – THE TOURISTS

The people that lived and worked in the castle were an absolute joy to meet. House cleaners, cooks, workers and scientists greeted them warmly as they walked around the massive building. The modern elements of the castle blurred the lines between past, present, and future. The floors and walls were warm to the touch and there were digital monitors stationed on each wall. In the basement, they found a garage loaded with exotic cars. They looked in several unoccupied rooms and found each one was decorated with rich modern styles.

It didn't take much coaxing to convince Joslyn to stay for dinner at the castle and a quick cell phone call to her dad made sure it was ok. James was showing them around the upper floors when they wandered into a large entertainment room. They had walked in to take a closer look at the high-tech toys when they noticed a long pair of gangly legs poking out from behind a large wooden cabinet.

"Ah ha!" The muffled voice came from behind the cabinets.

"Ahem," James cleared his throat.

A tall lanky teen appeared from behind the center and waved at them. His sandy blonde hair was short and curly and there was a mischievous twinkle in his blue eyes. Indy immediately liked him.

"Hey James," the teenager said. "I got the PlayStation working. The HDMI cable had to be..."

The teen cut off when he noticed Indy and Joslyn standing behind James.

"Joslyn, Indy," James said. "This is Jon Lucas, our friendly neighbourhood techie. I believe you met his father at the front gates earlier."

Indy and Joslyn waved in greeting as the cell phone at James waist chirped loudly. James brought it to his ear in one fluid motion.

"Yes," he said and listened for a moment. "I am on my way sir."

"I need to go see your father Indy," he said and then waved Jon over. "Jon would you mind showing our guests around."

"Sure, no problem James," Jon said.

James nodded once and strode from the room.

"He's a really busy guy," Jon said as he packed his gear into a black backpack. He finished stuffing the bag with a jet blue iPad and walked over to them in the doorway.

Jon held out his hand and Indy shook it with a firm grip.

When Jon held out his hand to Joslyn, she remarked, "You know you have dirt on your face... right there."

Jon wiped it away and smiled weakly at her. "Anyway... I was just heading down to the kitchens for a late lunch," he said. "I guess that's as good a place to start as any."

They walked back the way they had just come and took one of the many concrete staircases down to the kitchens. They could smell the delicious flavours in the air, as they got closer to the kitchens.

Fresh bread was baking in the ovens as they walked in. Jon walked them into the large room where several women in aprons were kneading dough. He introduced them to the cook, Maggie Miles. Indy thought it was funny that Maggie looked a lot like Wendy from Flo's Diner. Joslyn even had to do a double take. The large grey haired woman swirled and danced through the kitchen as she tended to several different cooking pots at once.

"Hey Maggie? You got a sec?" Jon called as Maggie came twirling toward them.

Maggie smiled at Jon as she pulled him in for a large hug and a quick kiss on the cheek.

"Jonathan, you are practically skin and bones. Doesn't your father ever feed you? You kids need a little something to eat? I have just the thing for you."

She waved them all over to a large table in the corner as she went to work. The large aproned woman had packed them a quick picnic in no time and ushered them out the side door.

"You kids go find a nice little place to eat this snack," she said giving Jon another warm embrace. "Come back anytime kids, my kitchen is always open."

The parking lot outside the kitchen was empty of cars. Instead, there were ten side-by-side ATVs in the parking spots. A couple of the ATVs had full enclosures while the others were open-air models. They all had serious off road tires and rugged looks.

"Whoa," Indy exclaimed. "Does everyone get to ride around in those?"

"Yup," Jon said. "They are first come first serve but your dad ordered a fleet of them for the castle grounds. There are a lot of buildings across the campus and it makes it a lot easier to get around."

They walked up to an ATV with four seats and Jon slid behind the wheel.

"Hop in guys," he said.

Indy called shotgun and hopped in beside Jon.

Joslyn came around to the driver's side and asked Jon. "Can I drive?"

"Well maybe on the way back," Jon said. "This thing has an awful lot of power and we might see a bit of rough road around the back forest. I don't want you to get us stuck."

Joslyn sniffed at him and got into the back seat without another word.

Jon smiled wickedly and started the ATV. The kart rumbled softly as Jon gave it a bit of gas. The Razor surged a couple times as Jon brought it roughly around the side of the castle. The roads were paved and wide but they managed to drift onto the grass several times, as Jon waved his hands and pointed at the buildings and people they saw. Jon pointed out several low squat buildings in the distance before they came to a low rise.

"Your father has designed this section of the grounds as a sort of summer camp. He was telling my dad that he wants to have a place for everyone's kids to come during the summer months or even to open it up to kids in the surrounding towns. The camp is ready to go and some of your dad's companies have already scheduled company retreats here."

Jon began to gesture around the grounds again as the car started to weave across the grass. "There are the cabins over there and the athletic fields over there. There are a couple equipment sheds and a pool too."

They could see several kids playing a game on the soccer field.

"What kind of game are those kids playing?" Joslyn asked.

"They call it king's court," Jon replied. "It's really just dodge ball though."

"Why are they wearing hockey helmets?" Joslyn asked.

"Yea, well a couple of the older kids are a little rougher than they should be. After my friend Allen almost broke his nose, Mrs. Locke made it a permanent rule. No helmets, no game," Jon shook his head at the memory. "It really only seemed to make the games even rougher though."

The Razor kart zipped past the game and they could see one well-muscled youth without a helmet taunting a fallen player.

Jon pointed at the group and said. "That's Allen on the ground and that jerk without the helmet is Warren Hocking."

They watched as Allen tried to stand. Warren started to laugh as he pushed Allen back down.

"Don't they have a referee or something?" Joslyn asked as a worried expression crossed her face.

Jon shook his head. "There is supposed to be a volunteer councillor watching over the game but he is usually too busy hanging out at the pool with his girlfriend."

"Stop the kart," Indy said flatly. Indy was out and moving before the Razor came to a full stop. When the tires screeched on the pavement Warren looked up. He watched carefully as Indy came storming onto the field.

"Let him up," Indy growled.

"Mind you own business new kid," Warren said. "It's part of the game."

"Ya well, it looks like he doesn't like your game. So let him up," Indy said staring into the kid's dark brown beady eyes.

"Sure thing," Warren sneered. "How about you take his spot, since he doesn't want to play or are you chicken?"

The game around them stopped, all the kids lying on the ground or on the sidelines got to their feet and formed a circle around the pair of them.

Warren stood almost a foot taller than Indy and had a few more pounds on his thick frame too. Indy was smaller but in really good shape, thanks to his uncle. His uncle Brad Locke ran a mixed martial arts dojo near Indy's boarding school in Pebble Beach, California. Indy spent some of his free time working out with the fighters there, so he wasn't afraid to get a little rough. They stood there glaring at each other, neither one willing to look away.

Indy balled his fists and nodded. "Fine, let's do it," he growled.

"Warren!" A voice yelled harshly through the crowd. It came from an older man in a white lab jacket who had pulled up in a side-by-side ATV.

"Get in the kart," The man said. "Your father needs you down at the plant."

Warren sneered at Indy. "This isn't over. Come back tomorrow and we can play then."

The crowd broke apart to let Warren through and then began to wander away.

"You ok Allen?" Jon asked. Jon was there helping him with his battered helmet, trying to get the straps free of the mangled cage.

"What was that all about?" Indy asked Allen.

"Oh, it's just Warren again. He said he was bored and wanted to change the rules. Now when you get hit in the head you are supposed to lie down and stay down."

"That sounds a bit harsh," Joslyn said.

Jon introduced them. "Allen, this is Indy and Joslyn."

"Nice meeting you, thanks for the help too," Allen said as he brushed himself off.

"No problem Allen, I can't stand bullies." Indy was still running high on adrenaline.

"Are you going to play with us tomorrow?" pleaded Allen.

"Sure, that sounds like fun," Indy said with an evil grin. "You're going to have to teach me the rules though."

"Ok but later," Jon cut in. "I'm getting hungry and we haven't even seen half the grounds yet."

"See ya Allen" Jon waved to his friend and the rest of the kids on the field.

When they got back to the ATV Jon pulled out a map that was tucked away in the glove box and handed it to Indy. Jon pointed out several highlights they should explore as they looked over a map of the valley.

There was the experimental hydro station with its offshore wave catchers. A cliff side grouping of water caverns and blow spouts. Down in the valley there was a vineyard and orchard to top off the list along with acres of forest and mountain trails. Jon pointed out a small river that bordered the southern edge of a map. However, that area was flooded and was pretty much a large bog now. He suggested keeping away from it for the time being.

Jon steered the kart towards the woods as they decided to head towards the hydro plant.

"Hang on!" Jon warned.

Within minutes, they were bumping along a dirt track that swerved through some heavily wooded areas. They splashed through mud and drifted around corners. Indy and Joslyn shared several worried glances as they rushed through ever worsening terrain.

"Maybe you should slow down a bit Jon, the mud looks like it's getting deeper," Joslyn pleaded.

"No way," Jon said. "I know this path like the back of my-" The kart swerved suddenly and skidded to a stop in a deep bog of watery mud. The kart tires spun freely in the deep muddy ruts when Jon tried to get them free.

"Damn mud," Jon said. "We are stuck really good."

Joslyn told him she knew how to get them out. She tried to talk him through getting them unstuck but he just ignored her and kept tapping the throttle. She finally gave up waiting for him to listen and tapped him on the shoulder.

"My turn," she insisted as she climbed over the seats and into the front.

"Fine but it's not going anywhere," Jon huffed as he tried to make room for her.

They ended up switching seats and Joslyn shifted the machine into four low, and eased onto the throttle. Within seconds, they were out.

"Lucky I sat back here," Jon said. "We must have needed a little shift in balance to get us out."

They all had a good laugh as the kart zipped along the path.

Jon pulled out the map again and leaned into the front seats to show Indy. Jon made a large circle with his finger that traced the center of the valley around them.

"Last night my dad showed me a map like this one," Jon said. "He warned me to stay inside this area. He said something about that group of scientists Mr. Locke called in to survey the valley. I guess they have found some pretty strange stuff."

Indy was instantly intrigued. "What kind of strange things?" he asked, not knowing if Jon knew about the white staff and its strange effects or not.

"I guess they were saying that everything inside this circle seemed to grow a bit larger than normal. It is as if the whole area has been fed large doses of miracle-gro. My dad was also saying that several groundskeepers have reported huge rabbits too. They were complaining that the grounds were really getting torn up in several places."

"That sounds a little farfetched doesn't it? I mean really, giant rabbits?" Joslyn laughed hard at that. "Maybe he was just pulling your leg and trying to keep you close to home, after all Northern California also sees the occasional mountain lion and the odd bear too."

Jon pointed to the can of bear spray under the dash. "Speaking of bears, those were put there just in case," he said. "Your dad thinks of everything."

The Razor ATV tore across the hillside and then across the upper valley ridge before heading down toward the hydro plant. Joslyn was a good driver and Indy felt a lot safer and happier with her driving. They bounced down a steep slope and skidded down through the sands of the coast before heading back up the ridge to the seaside blowholes. Several giant jets of water shot up into the air as they went by. Mist from the water soaking their faces as they raced by.

Jon spoke up from the back seat. "I'm really getting a bit hungry. Why don't we stop over there to eat?"

"Ok, that's sounds like a good idea. With all the excitement I forgot I was hungry," Indy said.

Joslyn laughed as the Razor skidded to a stop at the edge of the woods. They parked near a large redwood tree and pulled the basket from the back of the ATV.

Jon spread out a blanket he found in the back of the ATV and soon their feast was set.

"This place is beautiful," Joslyn said as she looked around.

Indy nodded and pointed out to the sea. Another chopper was making its way towards the castle.

"My dad just can't sit still," he said. "Even here in his so called retirement home he found a way to keep busy.

As they tucked into their picnic lunch, they watched a flock of seagulls sailing in the wind. In the distance, the air seemed to waiver like heat haze. It reminded Indy of the shimmering aurora they had passed through this morning.

"Can you guys see the lights in the air over there?" What do you think it is?" Jon asked the question that had been on Indy's mind. "Do you think it has anything to do with that staff your mom's carrying around?"

"Wait a sec," Indy said as he looked at Jon. "What do you know about that staff?"

"I'm not sure what it is, but I know that it's something pretty sweet," he said. "Your mom healed my dad's knee a few days ago and I was there to see it. The staff had this weird blue light… my dad's knee used to be so bad he could barely walk. Now he can run again.

Indy told Jon about the car accident and the resulting injuries his mom suffered. Then the heartbreaking news of cancer that stole her strength that followed.

"My mom had been in a wheelchair for years and the doctors said she would never walk again," Indy said. "But because of the staff, she has recovered almost completely."

"It might be magic but either way she is the happiest I have ever seen her," he continued. "But there is something else I noticed," he told Jon about the ring of tall grass they had seen when they came in on the bike earlier that day. "There was this… heat haze over the road and it kinda did something to me."

"What are you talking about?" Jon asked.

"On our way in today my bike stalled. We got off to check things out," Indy said. "Well, I felt something just after we got off the bike. It was like a fire burned right through me."

He reached up to his neck. "I was wearing a crystal dragon on this necklace," Indy said. "When the feeling was gone so was the dragon."

"That's so weird," Joslyn said, looking at him a bit sideways. "I felt a bit of static electricity when I got off the bike but I didn't think much of it at the time.

Jon pulled out the map. "Show me where it happened," he demanded and handed over the map. They both looked at the map as Indy traced the road that ran from Appleton to the castle. He put his finger on the spot the bike had stopped. Jon leaned over and made a circle with his finger. It ran right over the spot Indy had pointed out.

It was just inside the ring his father had drawn.

"I would guess that the line of growth we saw continues around the complete perimeter following that circle," Joslyn said as she looked thoughtfully at the map.

"So what do you think is causing it?" Jon asked.

"I don't know what it is but..." Indy pointed at the orchard dead center of the circle. "My guess is we will find the answer here."

"Ok then, why don't we head down there and check it out... right after we eat," Jon suggested.

They all sat down on the blanket and tucked into the meal with gusto.

It happened so fast there wasn't anything they could have done. Indy saw Jon look up into the tree behind them, his mouth forming a silent oh. Indy was eating with his back to the tree and the next he knew he was pinned beneath two hundred pounds of tearing teeth and claws. His face hit the ground first. His head was pushed down hard against the ground and he couldn't see anything except dirt and grass. He didn't even feel a thing.

The moment of shock passed and Indy began to fight back. He spun under the mountain cat and grabbed it by the throat. Fangs bit at him but nothing sank in his flesh. The big cat had bits of his shirt in its mouth, as Indy looked the cat in the eyes. His hands began to squeeze the big cat's throat as they rolled around.

"Indy!" he heard Joslyn yell.

A blast of foam hit the cat and splattered over his own face. The bear spray coated the big cat almost as much as it did himself.

The result was instant, for the cat at least.

It hissed and spat but sprang away into the dense bushes and left Indy sprawled out on the ground.

"Are you ok?" Jon and Joslyn asked at the same time. Joslyn had run back to the kart and was running at him from the back of the Razor with a first aid pack in her hand.

Jon was standing over him with the can of bear spray in his hands.

Indy's shirt was shredded and his jeans had long tears showing through to his muscled legs. Amazingly, he didn't have a single scratch on his skin.

Indy stood up, ripped his tattered shirt off his back, and used it to wipe the foam from his face. Not even the foam bothered him one bit.

He held one hand up to stop Joslyn from tearing apart the first aid kit.

"I'm ok, it didn't even scratch me," he said as he finished wiping the foam away.

She stood slack jawed staring at him. "Indy... Your chest... The tattoo... It moved."

"Tattoo? What are you babbling about I don't have any..." he looked down at his chest and sure enough, he had a large black sinewy dragon on his chest. It was black as night with bright red eyes. The eyes seemed to look up at him as he looked down.

"What the hell is that?" yelled Jon.

They came closer to look at the swirling black tattoo. Joslyn reached out to touch it. The dragon swirled away from her touch, moving in a ripple around Indy's back.

Indy looked in her eyes as her hand rested on his bare chest a moment longer.

That moment was shattered by the buzz of a helicopter. It blew by overhead and settled in for a landing a hundred feet from them.

A large bald man jumped from the door as the copter touched down. He was dressed in a black shirt and camouflage pants and was carrying a large hunting rifle.

"Are you kids ok?" the big man asked. "We got an emergency signal from your ATV. We got here as soon as we could."

"We're ok Zeus," Jon said as he looked at Indy and Joslyn then back. "A mountain lion knocked Indy down but we scared it off with the spray before it could hurt anyone."

Indy recognized the man with the grey-eyed glare. Zeus was head of security for the Locke's and Indy had several confrontations with the man previously. The man didn't have an ounce of humour in his whole body. Indy couldn't ever remember seeing the man smile let alone laugh.

"Ok kids," Zeus was saying. "I have to report it though, every can of that spray is logged, and every incident has to be investigated. You guys are just lucky we were doing overhead security sweeps."

Zeus keyed his earpiece. "Stand down, Repeat stand down. We have a mountain lion sighting on the ridge southeast of hydro one. No injuries to report."

He turned back to the kids. "We've had several other incidents this week," he said as he held up his hand as another call came over the radio earpiece. "Yes sir. No sir," he looked closer at Indy. "He is right here sir. Right away."

"Mr. Locke requests you return to the castle as soon as possible, junior. Would you like to ride back in the heli?" he said it with a flat deadpan voice as his beady eyes glinted.

A sour looked crossed Indy's face. He was sure Zeus knew he didn't like heights or flying. Anytime he absolutely had to travel by plane, he had a doctor prescribe tranquillizers.

"We were just heading back," Indy said tightly. "If you really need to babysit me, you can try to keep up."

Indy nodded at the others and he bolted to the Razor and hopped in. His friends were only steps behind. Joslyn threw the kart into gear and hammered the gas. Dirt sprayed at the security guard as they ripped across the grounds heading back to the castle.

Zeus was a little slower getting back to the helicopter but was quickly after them. The helicopter trailed in their wake as they raced back to the castle.

EDEN 4 – SPY KIDS

The first thing Indy did when he got back to the castle was to find his way to his private rooms. He needed to be cleaned up and changed. A headache was pounding between his eyes and it was starting to affect his mood. He had agreed to meet Jon and Joslyn back in the entertainment room when he was done. As he showered clean, he continued to think about the lion attack and the fact that the cat didn't hurt him. The big cats teeth had wrapped around his face and his clothes were shredded. How could he not have been hurt?

Indy stepped from the steamy shower to stand in front of the large mirror over the sink. He brushed the steam away from the mirror with a towel and looked at his reflection. Bright green eyes stared back at him under a mess of wavy brown hair. His bare chest glistened with moisture from the shower but he couldn't see the tattoo he had glimpsed earlier.

He was just about to turn away when the dragon came rippling around his torso and stopped just above his heart. After catching his breath, he looked closer at the dragon. The fine detail of the tattoo amazed him. Tiny scales, teeth, and horns rippled over its skin. Breath even seemed to spill from its slightly opened mouth as he watched. Indy raised his fingers to his chest. The dragon stayed in place as Indy ran his finger along the beast, tracing its form around his chest.

41

He thought he could feel a warmth beneath his hand before the dragon darted away again. Indy stared into the mirror a long while before he finally dried off. He dressed in a new pair of jeans and an old Guns and Roses shirt before heading downstairs. He considered the dragon as he found his way back to his friends. That dragon along with the news of his mom's recovery was making this certainly a day to remember.

Over the next few hours, the kids played video games, ate a pizza, and watched a movie. All thoughts of the lion attack had left Indy's mind as they enjoyed each other's company. Joslyn called her dad to make sure it was okay to visit overnight, she made sure to leave out any details of the dragon tattoo, or lion attack. It took a few minutes of convincing but in the end her dad relented when he found out she was a guest of the Locke's and staying in the guest wing. She was allowed to stay overnight but there was a catch, she had to agree to take her sisters lunch shift at the diner the next day.

Joslyn and Jon bickered over the movies they wanted to watch. Jon wanted something fast and exciting while Joslyn wished to see an emotional heartthrob movie. They ended up watching a young wizard battling a dragon.

After the movie had finished they began chatting about their lives. Indy related the horrors of private boarding schools and his father's plea for him to take a year off school to live in the castle with them. Joslyn recounted growing up in Appleton as the daughter of a sheriff in a small town.

When they turned to look at Jon for some insight into his life, he broke out an iPad and waved it at them. After a few quick finger taps, they were watching the iPad being displayed on the room's big TV screen. Jon told them how much he enjoyed computers and all things techie. They laughed and called him a geek.

"I've been here since they first started wiring this place," Jon said. "My dad took me around to watch them work after I begged him a few thousand times. A couple of the techs showed me a few little tricks and anyway... check it."

The big screen lit up with images. There were views of the castle that Indy recognized. There was the grand hall, dad's personal car storage, the garage and the kitchen.

"That's incredible," Indy said as he leaned closer for a better look.

"It's very invasive," Joslyn said with a sniff.

"No, it's not," Jon said. "Look there's no bathrooms and no bedrooms here, just the public areas."

Jon tapped a couple of the images and they enlarged to fill half the screen.

"These cameras are really great, I can zoom in, see in the dark, and record anything I see," Jon said proudly.

Jon swiped at the two images on the iPad and they began to flick through a random rotation.

"Look that's us," Joslyn said pointing at the screen.

Jon stopped the screen and they watched themselves watching the TV.

"Ya, once I saw that feed, I moved the room around so the cameras can't see the TV screen," Jon said.

"Can it hear us?" asked Joslyn.

"Nope these cameras don't have any microphones equipped, but watch this," Jon did a quick double tap and the images shifted. The screen blurred through different filters, night vision, and then heat vision before it started to zoom in. It can track motion too."

Joslyn stood up, walked over to the corner, and looked around carefully.

The image showed Joslyn as she moved closer to the wall. Her pretty blue eyes filled the screen.

"I can't even see the camera," she said frowning. "Where is it?"

"I'm not supposed to know but I had a talk with Sasser. He is the castle's tech guy and resident watchdog." Jon said grinning wide. "The camera is tucked back into the wall. Only a small coloured lens is visible. Anyway, he told me all about the castle's little extras, the hidden rooms, and the secret passages. I guess your dad is really big into hiding stuff too."

"Ya," Indy said nodding slowly. "A few years back we had some sensitive equipment stolen. One of our products was leaked before the thing could hit the market. Some Chinese company reverse engineered it and it came out the day after ours. My dad lost millions of dollars because of it."

The screens started scanning again and the orchard popped up, Jon zoomed in. "This is what I wanted to show you. I've been here for months now. But this camera screen was added about a week ago."

The camera showed rows and rows of apple trees and in one far corner sat a country store.

"That's Hanks place," Joslyn said. "He's a friend of my dad's. Hank's store has the best cider I've ever had."

A long driveway led through the orchard to the parking lot.

"I don't remember that section of parking lot though," Joslyn said, as she looked closer at the lot. "Look there," she said.

A far section of the lot was sectioned off and a tiny sign said, "Caution. Sink hole."

"That must have happened after the big electrical storm and flooding right?" she asked.

"Yup," Jon said. "I've seen a lot of stuff like that since then. After the storm, a science team landed and setup shop in the plant. They have been buzzing around the valley gathering data. I heard a few of the talking about solar radiation and the Ionosphere."

"Hey, you still have that map from earlier?" Indy asked.

"Nope, I left in the Razor. No worries though, I can bring up Google earth on my iPad," Jon brought up the satellite view of the valley and overlaid a rough circle overtop it all with the tip of his finger.

"I think I was right, that little sinkhole looks like it would be dead center of the circle," Indy said with certainty.

"You know what else was weird, now that I think of it. Around the same time as the scientists came in your dad started acting a bit... odd. He started shipping in old crystal artwork by the crateful. It's as if he had gone on some kind of wild random shopping spree.

Indy nodded. "My dad sent me up here with a backpack full of crystals from our old attic. What do you think he is looking for?"

Indy thought about the black dragon crystal and answered his own question, "It has to be something about the crystals. The dragon tattoo on my chest looks a lot like the crystal pendant I had on and my father was gathering up all the crystal he could find. That has to be it. But I wonder why."

"I bet some of the crystals are magic," Joslyn said.

"No way," Jon said flatly. "Magic is just a way to describe technology you don't understand yet. So this stuff is obviously tech."

Indy looked from one friend to the other as they stared at each other. Neither one was going to be willing to back down from their stance on the issue. So Indy redirected. He lifted his shirt to reveal the tattoo and said. "So does this make me a super hero?"

A grin spread across Joslyn's face as she considered it for a moment. "Let's find out shall we," she said. The grin on her face should have told him she was up to no good.

The pillow whipped across from behind her back. It hit so hard it nudged his face to the side but he didn't feel a thing.

A smile spreading across his face but disappeared as a thick hard covered book came next. An Xbox controller ricocheted off the back of his head as Jon joined the fray. The battle ended when a pool cue came crashing down on his shoulder. The stick shattered and splinters flew everywhere.

"Anything?" they asked.

Indy's smiled grew even wider. "Nothing," he said as he brushed some splinters off his clothes. "I can feel the pressure of something hitting me and even some of the texture of what was hitting me. But I felt no pain. The impact moves me a bit, but that's it."

Jon stepped closer with a balled fist. The roundhouse came quicker than he expected and the impact rocked Indy's head back.

"My hand!" Jon screamed. Jon was cradling his hand but had an awed look in his eyes. "Anything that time?"

"Nope." Indy's grin became contagious.

"Hmmm," Joslyn's eyes sparkled with curiosity and she held up a small pocketknife she had slid from her pocket. "I don't think I can do this part," she said softly. She handed the slim blade to Indy, hilt first.

He stared at the knife for a long second before putting the blade to his palm. Before he could even try to slice his flesh, a dark form poked its head out from under his sleeve. The dragon swirled out and placed its body beneath the blade. It red eye glowed as it stared back at him.

Indy pressed the slim blade hard against his flesh. The blade moved but did not cut the skin beneath. The dragon continued to stare up at him a moment longer before sliding away.

They looked around at each other mystified and awed.

Then sirens went off before they could discuss it any further. The wailing sirens blasted over an intercom in the hall. Running feet pounded outside their room. Shouting came from just beyond the door.

"He's on the roof." They heard a gruff voice say. "All units listen up. We have a thief. Hulk and Macke have chased him out onto the roof."

The voiced paused a moment as they listened intently at the door.

The voice spoke again, "Guards are reporting a missing patient from the hospital wing. He knocked out an orderly and ran."

Another voice broke in just then, "He's on the ground now and moving fast. What the... he just scaled the outer wall. The guy is moving like a damn cat, he is over top now. It looks like he's heading toward the quarry's train tracks."

A deep rumbling voice responded. It was Zeus again. "Get the jeeps out and track him down. Markus. Get the chopper up and provide air support. Swing a couple units down the main road to the quarry as well. Cut him off before he gets to the main road."

"Move it!" Zeus screamed.

Zeus must have been right outside their door. They heard him switch channels and call for Doc Hocking. "Doc. Come in Doc."

"I hear you Zeus. This is Doc."

"We have a breach sir. One of the patients from the hospital wing has gone missing. We just got word that it's Hans, sir," Zeus reported.

"The man with the gloves?" Doc's voice sounded pained.

"Yes sir," Zeus confirmed.

"Keep me updated Zeus," Doc said. "I want those gloves back a.s.a.p."

"And Hans?" Zeus asked.

"Do whatever it takes but make sure he does not make it outside the aurora," Doc said coldly.

"Yes sir. Zeus out."

They could hear the large man as he moved down the hall.

"They are pretty serious about getting this guy back," Jon said.

"No kidding," Joslyn added. "I would hate to be that Hans guy right about now."

Indy chuckled... and a wide grin spread over his face. "I could just imagine the look on Zeus's face if I brought back this guy instead of one of his teams. It would serve him right for..."

Indy stood abruptly and the smile turned into an evil grin. He produced a Bluetooth earpiece from his pocket and gave Jon the number.

"Jon, break out that iPad of yours. I need you to try to track this Hans person with the cameras. Keep me updated on my cell phone. I'm going to take my bike and see if I can get ahead of those jeeps. If I'm not back in thirty minutes tell my dad where I went."

"Indy, don't go," Joslyn begged and grabbed him by the arm. "I've got a bad feeling about all this... stuff. We still don't know enough about the situation."

Indy gently lifted her hand from his arm.

"Don't worry guys, nothing can even scratch me. What could possibly go wrong?" Indy winked at them. He turned to open the entertainment room's balcony doors and hopped up onto the railing outside.

He was on the second floor and made the jump without even thinking. He dropped over twenty feet down to the ground. Indy landed on his feet and rolled through the fall. Dust flew around his feet as he scrambled around the front of the main building.

His Ducati was right where he left it. He hopped on the motorcycle and roared away, his unneeded helmet spinning on the ground. The main gate was just closing as he followed a couple of security jeeps through. He squeezed through just in time waving at Barney as he passed. The jeeps turned right and took the quarry road, heading down hill. Indy recalled on the map the high ridge road led to a set of train tracks that led straight down into the quarry.

The Ducati turned left and raced through the clear night. He pulled off the road when he spotted the tracks. A quick turn and a little more throttle and he was up and then between the track rails. Dark woods surrounding the tracks on either side raced by as he poured on the speed.

His Bluetooth rang.

"Jon?" he asked clicking on the earpiece.

"Ya Indy. Nothing's changed, they are still tracking Hans into the quarry yard."

Overgrown weeds and branches thumped off Indy and the bike as he thudded down the tracks between the rails. The tracks here were overgrown with branches and weeds. They must not have been used since the last stones had been carved and carried up the hill on them months ago. The tracks were angling down now, following the edge of the ridgeline. He could just make out the quarry buildings in the distance. Somewhere ahead a helicopter stirred the air.

The bike came to a stop beside the quarry train and he shut down the engine to listen. He could hear the night come alive around him as the Ducati's engine ticked quietly from the abuse of the hard ride. Ahead the chopper was circling the quarry using a big spotlight to search the ground. He could already see headlights from the jeeps shining through the trees. They were getting closer but still a ways off. At the far end of the quarry was the road leading to Appleton.

Indy was thinking to himself. "He's gonna have to try for the road before the jeeps get here or else he will be trapped." Indy reached down to start the bike when he heard a noise behind him. Someone was behind him, following him on the tracks.

"Behind you Indy!" Jon's warning came too late.

A man stepped from behind the train and walked towards him. "Nice bike," the man said from the shadows. "Now just get off it real slow and back away."

The man walked closer and flicked his hands out to either side. His hands looked like oversized tiger paws complete with an opposable thumb and... Claws.

The man growled at him and said. "I'm not sticking around this nut house to be someone's lab rat."

Without warning, he pounced on Indy. Large hands gripped Indy's shoulders and he was ripped off the bike. After being lifted high in the air, he was tossed casually to the side.

"Stay down kid," Hans said. "If you're smart you should take the first chance you get to get away from here too. That Doc Hocking is a monster like none I had ever seen."

With that, he started the bike.

Indy rose to his feet.

"You are nothing but a thief," Indy yelled at him. "If you don't want our help... fine, leave. But I am not letting you leave with those gloves or my bike."

Hans laughed. "You don't get it do you kid," he held a paw up for him to see. "Ya they were once a pair of gloves, until I put them on. After a while, I started to... change. Not just my hands but my hair and eyes too. When I finally saw myself in the mirror, I asked to take them off. I begged them to let me take them off. They said no, they needed to learn more, always more. They strapped me to a bed when I threatened to leave. They tranquilized me after I managed to free myself the first time. I can't take these damn things off without someone else's help. I've tried everything I could think of but I can't seem to grip them with these... claws."

"Indy those jeeps are almost at the quarry now," Jon said into his earpiece.

Indy could just barely hear their engines churning in the distance.

Hans could hear them too. "I'm leaving and if you get in my way, I WILL kill you," The man raised his claws so Indy could see them a little better.

The man in the hospital gown kicked Indy's bike into gear and gave the bike some throttle. The bike shot forward swerving around the train, heading into the quarry.

Indy might have been able to stop him. But, he saw the desperation in the man's eyes and heard the fear in his voice. Indy let him go.

He watched the bike as it made its way across the bottom of the quarry. Hans was almost to the far edge when the bike sputtered and crashed. Hans got up quickly and made to run. The man in the hospital gown began to glow faintly at first then seemed to explode with light. When the light dimmed Hans was still standing there but now he was a crystal statue.

The jeeps and chopper stopped just short of the fallen Ducati. The choppers blades slowed as it landed and Indy could hear the men's voices by some trick of the quarry's walls.

"Yes sir. He found a motorcycle somewhere and the bike went through the buffer zone. Hans turned to crystal about five seconds after that."

Indy couldn't hear the other end of the conversation but he could here Zeus's voice louder than before.

"Listen up men! Doc's recommending we quarantine the valley until we know exactly what's going on here. No one comes in and no one goes out. All ways in and out are to be barricaded and manned. All incoming choppers are being diverted to Appleton until further notice. Head back to base and we can setup your man assignments."

Indy crept back along the tracks moving slowly back towards the castle.

"Jon... Did you see that?" Indy asked into the Bluetooth.

"Ah, yeah... we recorded the last bit. Hans just froze as soon as he got outside the circle," Jon said. "Now he looks like a statue made of pure crystal."

EDEN 5 – BREAKING NEWS

The next few days passed by in a blur. Flights and deliveries into and out of the castle were diverted into the nearby town of Appleton. Daniel Locke, Sr. made every assurance to the people living in and around the castle that these were precautionary measures and only temporary. Both Mr. and Mrs. Locke urged voluntary compliance and even Doc Hocking spoke urgently to his science teams in order to prevent further incidents.

Still, after the barricades were raised on both roads into and out of the valley, people started to panic. Phone lines became jammed as people tried to contact their families and friends outside of the valley.

Daniel Locke was in constant contact with the sheriff's office in Appleton and other media sources. Sheriff McCloud organized similar checkpoints outside the barely visible shimmering aurora in order to help dissuade anyone else from entering the area. The castle's security forces stayed on top of the situation and even prevented several attempts to exit through the barricades. People were scared and frightened and the military type checkpoints around the grounds didn't help allay fears.

Some people felt the castle had become a prison while others agreed that the precautions were in place for their protection. The castle hallways soon became like a ghost town and the summer camp out back was even worse. Not a single solitary kid played on the courts or fields. Most had hidden themselves away in their rooms along with their parents.

It was a stroke of brilliance when James designed a system to get needed supplies into the valley without endangering any more lives. At the spot where the main road to Appleton met the aurora, he had a small team of workers to create a hands free method of bringing in food and supplies. The aurora of light only spanned a thickness of ten to fifteen feet so it was possible to push and pull long flatbed trailers through the area with bulldozers without the need for a person to cross into the curtain of lights.

The whole community was adjusting to the new situation when another wrench was thrown at them. The United States military forces began arriving later that day and started to raise their own barricades and support structures. Eventually a no-fly zone was initiated and maintained by a pair of f-14 jets.

Luckily, news sources were in place before any military blackouts could be instituted and a news conference was set for the following morning. The news agencies were assured that explanations and demonstrations would take place. The military warned against it but bowed to public pressure after several attempts to disrupt media access to the area inside the aurora resulted in several artifact experiment videos hitting the net.

It turned out that doctor Hocking, in great foresight had backed up all the video recordings of his findings so far to computers on an outside network. Along with the videos he had sent directions to upload select portions of it to YouTube should contact with his team be lost.

By then everyone had begun referring to the shimmering wall of air around the valley as the Aurora California. Since Indy's arrival the shimmering wall had grown much more visible at all times. It was a myriad of colors dancing and waving across the sky.

His father came to him in his rooms late that night as Indy lay trying to sleep. He told him that the next morning they were going to schedule a news conference and it was time that they share their discoveries with the world. His father was worried that even though they might not have all the answers yet, if they didn't say something soon the government might find a way to keep them all silent.

The next day the news conference was a zoo. Satellite news vans were spread out in long lines along both sides of the Appleton road. There were reporters interviewing anyone they could, farmers, civilians and even some government officials. The U.S. military was also out in full force. The no fly zone was heavily enforced and a pair of jets that did regular sweeps around the aurora of light. The two jets buzzed around the shimmering aurora and chased off several news helicopters that dared get too close.

Seating for the press conference had been pre-arranged and several rows of ranking military had seated themselves nearest the stage. Between the seats and stage, a row of soldiers had formed a solid line of bodies. They stood in front of a white line painted across the road. Behind them the aurora sat, with its slight haze, in the dawn light. Each soldier in line cradled an assault rifle and stared unmoving into the crowd, their backs to the aurora itself. Ten feet further towards the stage was another line, this one however was painted red. It divided the area before a large raised stage that was equipped with monitors and TVs.

The Locke's, James, Doc, and Zeus waited patiently in chairs placed across the back of the stage. Joslyn, Jon and several other castle dwellers waited in a small audience to one side of the stage.

Daniel Locke, Sr. took the stage first. The man stood solemn in front of the podium. When he spoke, his words were carried via speakers to the waiting crowd.

"Thank you all for coming," he said. "Please hold all questions until after we have finished. I know what you are about to hear may be considered unbelievable. It may even sound like the ravings of a mad man. I assure you it is not. Nor is this a parlour trick. Inside this shimmering aurora of air, you see before you, we have discovered an incredible source of power of unknown origins. We can and will, provide demonstrations and scientific data as evidence of our findings. My team and I are prepared to allow an international community of scientists' voluntary access to any and all artifacts and or technologies we have or may uncover."

Murmuring grew among the U.S. military personal and the news hounds pressed closer with their microphones and cameras.

Daniel Locke raised his hands requesting silence. "However new data has come to our attention and must be further analyzed before anyone will be allowed access to any of these uncovered items." Daniel paused as he looked around the stage and held his gaze on Doc Hocking for a moment. "My scientists have determined the area surrounding this valley is encompassed by an energy curtain. This field that we have come to know as the Aurora California. This aurora has grown in power in recent days since the initial discovery several weeks ago."

"Since that time we have had some rather disturbing news. An incident that occurred late last night has resulted in the possible death of one of my fellow workers. After spending several weeks in close proximity to these artifacts Mr. Hans Gretel decided to leave our valley. When Mr. Gretel passed through the aurora, his body became coated in a sort of crystal. At first, it appeared that he had frozen solid, but upon closer examination, his body was determined to have crystalized. His body is now in the possession of the U.S. military and they are trying to determine exactly what happened and whether or not the crystallization process is reversible."

"My team, working alongside the U.S. military scientists, have determined that it is incredibly dangerous for any person inside this field to exit through the aurora at this time."

The TV screens began showing images of Hans's crystal statue.

"The statue on the screens you see before you is Mr. Hans Gretel. This video is streaming live from a rock quarry north of this very spot. The crystallization occurred within seconds of passing through the aurora you see before you. The U.S. military scientists have secured this man's statue and are continuing to monitor his condition and run their own tests."

"They have agreed with our concerns and our suggestions. On both sides of this event we have taken measures to ensure the safety of all those in the area. For the time being, the area is sealed. No one will be permitted in or out of this area, for the time being. A no fly zone is also in affect to prevent an accidental airborne intrusion into the area."

Daniel looked towards his wife and smiled.

"We are however allowing several willing volunteers to come through at this time." Daniel Locke held up his hands before anyone could object or start asking questions. "These people have been carefully selected on certain merits and conditions. Each person has been made aware of the dangers of entering this area. Every patient that has been chosen is physically injured or terminally ill. They also are able to understand their choices and their possible results. Each person is also capable of entering the aurora without anyone's aid, so as not to endanger any more individuals then necessary."

"Our demonstration will be performed on each of these patients," Daniel said with a triumphant smile and waved to several men at the rear of his audience. "Please bring the volunteers forward now."

Dan motioned to Jolie and James to move to the side of the stage. As they did, he announced Doc Hocking. "Please welcome my chief medical and technical advisor, Doctor Henrik Hocking."

The doctor strolled to the podium shaking Daniels hand before taking over his spot at the podium. He started right in on the technical data. "Once we discovered the existence of this aurora's area of effect or AOE for short, we set about surveying and monitoring its output."

The overheads switched to an overhead map of the valley with a large red circle centered on the screen. "Friday night two weeks ago this area was hit by an electric storm of unknown origins. Due to this storm, the regions power grid shorted out and Appleton's largest dam had a catastrophic failure.   Further complicating matters unrelenting rains devastated many of the low-lying areas in the region.

Shortly after the massive electrical storm a visible aurora anomaly appeared.   This aurora appears to be very similar to its northern counterpart, the aurora borealis.   Typically, an aurora is caused by the collision of energetic charged particles with atoms in the high altitude atmosphere, in this case the Ionosphere.   The charged particles are generated from the magnetosphere and solar winds.   Once charged, these particles are gathered by the earth's magnetic field into the atmosphere.

The aurora surrounding this valley differs in that it is a constant non-moving event.   It has formed a perfect circle approximately twenty five miles in diameter.   The charged solar particles forming our aurora have somehow become further charged or altered by an unknown local event.   My team speculates this event is occurring somewhere in or around this valley.   In addition to the visible circular aurora, the air inside this circle has become charged as well.   The most basic comparison I can offer is that of an airborne battery."

Several technical slideshows started showing particles glowing and forming the waving aurora that surrounded them.

"During our investigations we have come across a large cache of artifacts that had been buried deep underground. These artifacts are all of unknown age and origins.   Typical carbon based scans and x-rays have revealed inconclusive data. It has proven impossible to investigate these items further.   In every case, the artifact turns to a crystal powder upon dissection of its outer shell.

However, my team and I have made some startling discoveries among these items.   It appears that some items we have found have changed or altered within this aurora. In some cases, it appears the molecular structure of each item has radically altered. In every instance these artifacts have displayed a startling effect."

"On the screens before us I have detailed on one such object," Doc pointed at the monitors where a long white staff twirled and rotated.

As Doc continued to talk, three patients had wheeled themselves through the crowd. Each person was a minor celebrity in one form or another. Tom Collins was a US Army Captain who had been paralysed by an I.E.D. in Iraq. Charlie Finds, a famous Rock Star with an advanced case of Aids. The last person in the group was a bit of a shock to everyone as she came wheeling through the crowd. Beatrice White, a well-known Actress in her nineties that recently had been hospitalized with a broken hip. The three patients had made their way through the crowd with orderly's escorting them. The crowd hushed as the three made their own way through the last few feet of aurora on their own.

Cheers erupted from the crowd as each crossed the threshold into the waiting care of the castle's medical attendants. Mrs. White struggled the last few feet in her wheelchair but pushed through to the cheers of everyone there.

The doctor continued as Mrs. Locke approached the trio. The staff the crowd watched on the overhead monitors was the same one she held in her hand. It was brilliant in the sunlight.

"So far we have found several artifacts in this area that are quite extraordinary. The single most visible one is the white staff that Mrs. Locke is holding now. As some of you may remember, Mrs. Locke had been restricted to a wheel chair after a horrific car accident a few years ago. After holding this staff for a number of days, we saw an incredible and unbelievable result. This wooden staff had begun to heal her. Both the cancer that had worn her life away and the lasting physical traumas of the accident she suffered. With the regenerative touch of this staff, she now walks unaided."

The white staff was being held by all four people now and a soft blue glow spread over them all. Each face was in awe of the power flowing through their body. Dark circles and sunken skin were replaced by healthy skin and bright eyes.

The doctor looked down at the four glowing people at the side of the stage. "In the first experiments after we realized the staff's potential it took much longer for any effects to become evident. We speculate that this artifact may have become attuned to Mrs. Locke and responds much quicker than before. What has taken hours before now takes..."

Beatrice was the first to stand. But the others followed quickly after her. They all held tightly to the staff as the doctor continued.

"...minutes."

Mrs. Locke nodded and the trio dropped their hands from the staff. The blue light faded and the cheers and murmuring grew louder. Several people in the crowd rushed forward but were held back by the soldiers.

The trio of patients were crying and smiling at the same time. They hugged Mrs. Locke in a fierce show of affection before stepping away and turning to greet the crowd. Cameras caught it all. The world would be forever changed by that one moment and the images caught there graced every paper and news source the world over.

Doc Hocking stepped quietly away from the podium with a hand to his heart. James looked slighted at the lack of introduction but took over the podium as the cheers quieted and the babble of voices increased. They all went silent as he raised his hand.

"With all this great news and excitement I hate to be the one to put a damper on this great day," he said.

"We have several unanswered questions that must be addressed. Concerning the fact, some people turn to crystal if they leave the area. We don't know if these people can be reanimated or how to do so safely. The crystal statue is hardened but breakable. It is impossible to know what would happen if the person is reanimated with missing or fractured pieces of crystal. We expect it would not be good if it were even possible. It is unknown at this time if it is the absence of the charged energy particles or the transition shell of the aurora surrounding this valley that causes this cellular crystallization."

"I want to stress one last point before we field some questions. We do not know how the aurora was formed or how it is being maintained. Our science team has found nothing to support many varied theories so far."

"Our biggest worry right now is what will happen to those within this crystal aurora should it fail."

Those people watching from the crowd hushed as the realization flooded through them.

"Our best guess would be that if the aurora fails every living creature under it would be instantly crystalized like our friend Mr. Gretel."

The crowd gasped and a wave of silence gripped everyone.

James continue after a long pause, "Until we know more the US military has imposed a quarantine zone. That is all we have right now. We can field a few questions now."

A dozen or more reporters put their hands in the air and Indy decided it was time to make an exit. He stepped away from the stage and walked to where Joslyn had gone after the demonstration. She was on her cell phone and waving to a group of people on the other side of the aurora.

A tall man in a sheriff's uniform was waving back along with an older woman with blonde hair and another younger woman that looked almost identical to Joslyn. A strong athletic blonde teenager was casting dark glares at him from just behind the sheriff's shoulder.

Joslyn looked up at Indy just then, tears in her eyes. She quickly wiped them away and introduced him to her family. Each waved to him until she introduced her father. The sheriff nodded and took the cell phone from his wife. Joslyn nodded as she spoke to her father and then handed the cell phone to Indy.

"My dad wants to speak to you privately," she said.

The sheriff had moved further from his family with the cellphone clutched in his hand. Indy took a few steps from Joslyn and raised the phone to his ear.

"Sheriff McCloud? he asked.

"Listen carefully Mr. Locke. My daughter is very special to us. You have put her in a very bad situation and because of this I am holding you solely responsible for her well-being." The sheriff's voice grew harsh and quiet. "I swear if anything happens to her you will regret it. I swear if anything at all happens to her I will personally come through these so called shimmering lights, in there after you."

"I understand sir," Indy said with a tight voice. He really didn't like being bullied but he understood the sheriffs concerns. "I won't let anything happen to her. I promise."

EDEN 6 – CAN I KEEP HIM?

The hydro plant gleamed in the suns fading light. Large glass windows, stone supports, and columns housed the most advanced hydroelectric wave capture plant in the world. Large waves from the Pacific Ocean crashed into the submerged tubular rotors generating mega-watts of energy.

The plant itself was an architectural beauty. Its real power was tied into an experimental geo-thermal energy storage system. The plant was up and running but only at a lower effective percentage due to some damage to the storage system suffered in the storm. The plant itself was still, but not quiet. In the days since the electric storm, things had changed drastically. Doc Hocking had been given free rein to experiment with the artifacts found in the orchard's underground vault. He and his team had converted much of the open space in the plant to suit their needs.

Inside, the building contained a lot of structural rock that had been allowed to intrude into the complex from the cliffs it was built on. Office space occupied the upper levels of the building and was connected via an overhead tunnel system. The overhead tunnel system ran from building to building as the complex flowed down the side of the cliff it rested upon all the way down to the coastal beach below.

The science team had reported that they had found nothing noteworthy except for the staff that Mrs. Locke wielded to heal. The tiger gloves that had disappeared with Hans had possibilities but like most other artifacts, they had discovered they could not divine any true power from them. In most cases, the artifacts displayed powers or effects that were uninspiring to say the least. With only a limited amount of artifacts and even fewer willing test subjects Doc Hocking was up against a wall.

Currently he was staring at a stand of possible artifacts and rows of animal cages in his lab, deep within the Hydro plant. Zeus came into the room cradling a large mountain lion in his arms. The large cat was sedated and unresponsive as Zeus deposited it into a metal reinforced cage. The big man slammed the door closed and stood to look at Doc.

"That's the last of the big boy's Doc," Zeus said as he wiped his hands on his dark blue guard's uniform. "If you need any more critters, your gonna have to ship them in from the other side. This little kitty was the last holdout. We haven't spotted anything larger than a rabbit for a couple days now."

"Thank you Zeus," Doc said as he came out of his daydream thoughts. "Come back in a few hours and while you're gone, see if any of our newest guests wish to be... helpful."

Zeus nodded and left the room leaving the doctor alone with his thoughts and the caged animals.

Henrik turned to his recording equipment and pressing a button, added a video log to his daily journal. "So far all of our experiments have shown that the creatures inhabiting this region have shown a slight increase in size. This may be in relation to their diets. Since most of the vegetation in the region has demonstrated a similar growth. None of the creatures examined have shown any outward sign of artifact powering. Blood samples have further confirmed this. The crystalline formations seen in human subjects that have come in contact with a powered artifact are not present in any animal species to date." The mountain lion interrupted his video log with a deep sullen growl. The doctor ignored it and continued with the log.

"Note - the shipment of primates anchored of the coast has been denied access to the docks and since has departed these waters."

The mountain lion growled again, the tranquilizer must have started to where off. That thought crossed Doc Hockings mind just as something else occurred to him. It was something about the cat, something about its growl. The way the noise didn't come from the other side of the room. It was right behind him. The doctor spun to find the lion atop a workbench almost eye to eye with him. It snarled at him and leapt.

Bang!

The beast barrelled into him, knocking him to the ground, and pinning the doctor under a dark furry mass.

"Doc you all right?" a voice called from above, it was Zeus. The weight eased off the doctor and he looked up. The large man had the dead body of the cat in one hand and a large calibre handgun in the other. Smoke drifted lazily from the end of the barrel.

"Yes. Quite," Doc said as he dragged himself to his feet. "Dispose of that thing and return here at once. We need to have a little talk about cages."

Zeus nodded and glared at him before leaving the room dragging the bloody corpse behind him.

"Pick that up before you make a bigger mess. Here use these," Doc said as he pulled a pair of large leather gloves from a belt at his waist and then threw them at Zeus. "On second thought don't come back. I've had enough interruptions for the day."

Zeus nodded and silently left the room with the large cat in his arms.

The lab was a mess, everything on the workbench was scattered on the floor in a heap. His notes and blood samples were smashed and his recording equipment had broken free of the AV racks and was scattered about the floor. He bent to retrieve the recording equipment and noticed several pieces were speckled with cougar blood.

"Great, I'm going to have to disinfect everything in here now," he said to the empty room. He scooped up the last of the recording devices but as he looked at it, he realized it was one of the artifacts. It was the large black box. When he first came across the box is had been just a plain wooden box, now it had blue runes that lit the surface. The box started to hum as he ran a finger over the blue symbols.

"Great... I was being so careful too," he reached one hand to his waist patting where the protective gloves normally rested. The gloves prevented skin contact with artifacts. Skin contact caused most artifact activations or effects. "Ah. What's done is done."

The doctor raised the box to look at it closer with his old brown eyes. The blue runes were pulsing slowly. The box began to hiss softly as the top started emitting light and a coloured gas. The gas swirled and flowed until it formed an image. It was some kind of three-dimensional light display. As the image formed in the air, two separate stands of DNA appeared. Each strand was displayed with amazing detail in the odd coloured gas. Below the image, each strand was labelled in the Latin format showing species and subspecies. Of the two DNA strands, one strain was clearly human and the other was that of a mountain lion.

"Fascinating," Henrik said.

The doctor poked a finger at the human strand of DNA and could feel his finger encounter the gas molecules. The image even moved slightly but held its shape like a solid object.

"Remarkable," he breathed.

He moved his finger with a little more pressure and the human strand moved across to the mountain lions side. Another push mounted the two strands atop each other. The image blurred and then reshaped with a new strand. A positive symbol and a negative lit below the new strand.

Doc nudged the plus sign.

The hissing continued and the DNA strand disappeared and was replaced with two new images. One was a man with lion-like face and the other was a lion with human hands but was completely furless. Each display had a flashing circle below it that was accompanied by a line of numbers.

"Now that's puzzling," Doc said to himself.

Then he poked the smaller of the two pictures, the image of a lion with hands.

The display zoomed into the lion and the same circle pulsed below it. He pushed the circle, the display stopped hissing, and the image dissolved like mist.

The box still pulsed and started to hum even louder. It was a sweet soft melody and the doctor caught himself nodding his head to its beat.

Doc stood and put the box on his workspace. He could see something that looked like dust blowing through several holes on the sides.

"Hmm. I don't remember those holes."

He was just about to turn from the box when the melody finished. The box opened and Doc looked in. A large crystal lay inside, cradled on a curved metal tray. Doc looked closer at the fist-sized egg. He could just make out the image of a small lion-man inside it. The little creature had incredible detail.

"It's a toy maker!" Doc exclaimed with the thrill of discovery. "Such fine detail, these would be worth a fortune if I could just get them off the grounds," he mumbled to himself.

He held the crystal egg up to the lights and a rainbow prism shone through.

"Yes!" A look of greed crossed his face as he looked around his large workspace. He walked over to a small row of cabinets and cleared out a space to hide the egg.

"You'll be safe here my little golden nest egg. Don't worry, I'm going to go make you some more friends. I don't want you to be lonely, do I?" The man's greedy grin only grew.

The doctor turned back to the black artifact box. Excitement shone clearly in his eyes as he put his hands to the box.

"I'm going to need some more blood samples," he grinned. "For testing purposes."

EDEN 7 – HANK'S HOLE

Daniel Locke walked into the entertainment room later that day as Indy was watching TV with Jon and Joslyn.

"Junior," he said. "I need a few moments of your time today."

He nodded at Joslyn and Jon then walked from the room without waiting for Indy to answer.

"Oh oh," Indy said. "He's in one of his moods… don't bother pausing the movie. I think I am going to be gone for a while."

"Ok," Joslyn barely looked at him and waved him out. She was concentrating heavily on the movie and a large bowl of buttery popcorn.

Indy caught up to his dad on the main stairs and walked beside him for a bit.

"What's up D?" Indy asked as they made their way down to the garage.

"Not here junior," Daniel said with a grin. "Let's go for a drive."

It was common knowledge among their friends and family that his father used driving as a tool to clear his head. All his clearest thoughts and brightest ideas came to him from behind the wheel of a car. They continued downstairs and down a back hallway to the rear of the castle.

They entered the garage and Indy looked around at all his dad's favourite rides. There was an Austin db7, Ferrari Enzo and his current favourite the Bugatti Veyron. Off to the side were his retired rides. There was the old Chrysler minivan where he dreamt up his first fortune 500 company. The old BMW M3 convertible he was in when he decided to buy into Google. Each retired car had some sentiment or an important decision tied to it. Each car was a story in itself.

The garage and all the cars inside were lovingly cared for by Scooter Barnes. Scooter was a pot-bellied mechanic they had met after their Minivan had died and left them stranded in the desert just outside Las Vegas. Back then, Scooter was in charge of a Luxury car rental company and had been joy riding in the desert when he spotted the ailing Minivan and the Locke family inside. Scooter had pulled over to help the vacationing family. That little piece of goodwill was something Indy's father had never forgotten. Years later, once their international shipping company was up and running, Scooter Barnes became one of the Locke`s first personal employees.

At the moment, Scooter was nowhere to be found but had left a car out for them that was gleaming in the garage's florescent lights.

The Veyron was their ride of choice that day. The million-dollar supercar was started with a push of a button as the father and son strapped themselves into the vehicle. They were through the open garage doors a few heartbeats later. The main gates were already open and they passed through and burst onto the pavement of the ridge road beyond.

The car stopped at the crest of the road with the valley opening up below them. The road in front of them was a black serpent twisting down the hillside.

His dad looked over at him as they sat there admiring the view. "I love you son. Sorry we haven't talked much since you got back. Things are a bit… hectic."

"I love you too dad," Indy said with a lopsided grin. "No worries, I know you're under a lot of pressure. Don't even think about it."

Obviously, his dad was thinking about it. The car squealed as they raced down the hill. Normally his father did these drives alone. So Indy was a little worried now that he was tagging along.

"So what's on your mind dad?" he said as they drifted through a long sweeping corner.

The corner came and went before his father spoke. "I just got finished speaking with the President of the United States. He's trying to make a play for control of the valley. There's quite a bit of pressure on us from other governments too. But so far, it's the U.S. that is making the most trouble for us right now.

They want all of our data and research along with inserting a team to oversee the work we will continue to do for them.

He actually ordered me to stop releasing any other data or news of any kind to anyone not in the U.S. military. Hell, he even said that they are looking to send a Colonel in here to run the day to day operations."

The car continued its smooth flight downhill.

His dad started thinking aloud as the car zipped down the hill. "I'm sure if they took over, everyone in here would be either bagged and tagged or put under a microscope for years.

75

I'm not ok with that." His father was silent for a few moments a thought turning behind his dark eyes.

"Me either," Indy said into the silence.

Daniel nodded absently and continued brooding.

His father started speaking again as the engine purred. "Luckily we have some friends in the international community and media. They have been essential in keeping the military out so far but I am afraid it won't last long. My supporters are caving and crumbling away from us."

"What are we going to do? How can I help? Whatever you need, you know I'm there for you dad."

"Thanks junior. I had a friend... actually, it was your uncle Brad, suggest something a bit crazy. I think might work but the timing just isn't right yet. We will need a lot of support and help to do it. It will be all or nothing." With any luck we may find a way to preserve this area from the rest of the world."

"Why dad? Why can't we share all this magic or technology with everyone? Imagine how many lives mom can save."

His father was shaking his head. "You don't understand junior. You haven't seen everything yet. The world isn't ready for what this place is or what it can do. There are people out there that if they got their hands on any of this stuff, the world could easily become hell. I can't tell you how lucky we are that so far none of this stuff works outside of this valley. From what Doc tells me, the aurora isn't going to get any bigger. So all of those fancy thingamajigs aren't going to do anyone any good outside this valley."

"So what is your Top Secret plan?" Indy asked.

"Wait for a bit," Daniel said. "I'm taking you to where it all started, where I found the artifacts and a few other interesting things."

The car pulled off the road at the orchards parking lot. Hanks store was down at the far end of the lot. At a guess the old man sitting on the porch was Hank. He sat there rocking back and forth on an old wooden chair. There was a large hound dog at his feet that sat up and barked as they pulled into a parking spot in the empty lot.

"Evening Hank," Daniel said as they got out of the car. "This is my son junior."

Indy waved as Hank stood from his chair. The man was a giant, easily six foot five and heavier than a bull.

Hanks voice was an avalanche of pure gravel as he spoke. "Evening Mr. Locke. Evening junior. I got some cider in the fridge if ya care to try some. Don't mind old snoop here, he's friendly."

Hank wandered into the store and they followed him in while Snoop chose to stay on the porch.

The old-fashioned store had rows of empty shelving but there were tons of small memento's and trinkets hanging from every available rafter and wall space. At the back of the store was a row of tall sliding glass coolers filled with bottles of a dark brown liquid. Hank had opened one such bottle and had three large cups poured by the time they got to the store's main counter. "Cheers," he said as he offered the cups.

They gulped the sweet drink and set the small cups down.

"Hank that stuff is awesome," Indy said.

"Thanks. It's my grandfather's recipe. Been in the family for generations. My wife's not with us anymore but she made a great pie that went well with the drink."

"Sorry to hear that, Hank," Daniel said.

"Why, don't you like pie?" Hank said with a little grin.

"No, I meant about your wife," Daniel said. Not sure if the joke was intentional.

"Oh," Hank said a full smile splitting his meaty face in half. "She was a great girl. But that's not why your here. You taking the boy downstairs Mr. Locke?"

Daniel nodded and together they both moved to either side of a barn door at the back of the store.

"Ready?" Daniel asked.

"Ready," Hank said.

They pressed their hands to price scanners on either side of the doors and within seconds, a section of flooring slid open at the center of the room. Lights winked on and stairs going down into the hole were illuminated.

"Welcome to the vault of Eden Indy," his dad whispered.

"Sweeeeet," Indy said as the breath rushed from his lungs.

They walked down the stairs and Hank watched them go.

Together they walked down carved earthen stairs into a well-lighted earthen room. The stone walls and floor were polished to a healthy dull glow. The room was empty and walls were bare of any coverings.

"Doc has everything that was down here over at the hydro station. For safety reasons we didn't want to bring anything untested into the castle," Daniel said.

"Sure dad," Indy said as he studied the room. "This is pretty cool."

His dad told him the complete story. How he found the tractor and the fall into the hole. All about the lightning storm that he may have had a part in. He told Indy about the artifacts that were in the room covered in a thick layer of dust.

"But here is the thing junior. I have been keeping a little secret. It's one the reasons I hesitate turning any of this stuff over. Stand back."

His father reached into a pocket and pulled out an ornate jewellery box.

"Really dad, you shouldn't have," Indy said in falsetto voice.

Daniel Locke ignored his son completely and opened the box with great reverence. A small human shaped panda bear jumped from the box to his open palm. It was dressed like a Japanese monk complete with wicker rice hat. The little guy stood about five inches high and moved with a sleek grace.

The bear bowed to his father and started a karate kata right there on his palm.

Indy was speechless.

His dad just grinned down at the swirling panda while it kicked and swatted at the air.

"Is he real?" Indy asked in a hushed voice.

"Yes, in manner of speaking. I ran a couple of tests on it. It doesn't bleed and I haven't seen it eat anything at all. In fact I'm not even sure it breathes."

"Who else knows about it?" Indy asked.

"Just you, James, Hank, and mom," Daniel said with a sly grin.

"Awesome," Indy said, not caring how it happened, instead being fascinated by the dancing bear. "Can I hold him?"

Daniel pulled his hand away quickly.

"Whoa. Not a good idea, junior. It's hard to explain but put it this way, he's kinda protective."

The box and panda were set carefully on the floor.

"Does it talk?" Indy asked as he tried to get a better look at it.

"Nope. Nothing outside a couple grunts and farts." Daniel laughed.

"Daaad, that's gross."

"Hehe. Sorry. But here is the last thing I need to show you," Daniel said in a more serious tone.

The panda monk ran around the room jumping and rolling around the vast space. He was a miniature whirlwind in the large room.

Daniel pointed at the closest section of wall and walked over to it. "Come over here and look at this, by the way how's your Latin?"

Indy came closer to the wall and peered intently at a large map of the world. The map had several large circular pictograms and a small scattering of Latin words. "Well, I can tell you it looks like Latin and it looks like they are names of different places," Indy smiled and shrugged. "That's about it."

Daniel Locke shook his head at Indy. "Ok well let me translate, you might recognise some of them already."

Daniel Locke's finger moved over the map and up the coast of California to the first label. "Eden." he said. As his finger moved over Norway, he said. "Valhalla." Over Greece, it was... "Olympus"

And so it went with several more labels each named something mythological or biblical in nature.

"Dad... These labels... They're all... places like this one, aren't they?"

Daniel Locke senior nodded a solemn agreement. "If it's true then this one little valley could be just the first of many. I have no idea when or how many of these places will become active, but we need to prepare. We need to be ready just in case," he turned to his son and looked deep into his eyes. "Are you with me son?"

"Yes," Indy replied.

"Then we must learn everything we can about this place and the things we found inside this room. The scientist I hired has not made any headway at all and to tell you the truth, I do not trust any of them. I want you to keep an eye on them and tell me if you hear or see anything that doesn't sit right with you. Trust me I have my reasons but I want you to come to your own conclusions."

Daniel Locke Sr. started to pace the room. "The walls in the castle have eyes and ears so be very careful who you talk to about this. I know that sounds a bit paranoid but my secured network has been compromised several times over the past few weeks and it makes me wonder what else might be going on around here."

Indy thought of Jon's little magic iPad but decided to keep it to himself for now. He nodded his head. "Sure, no problem dad. But can I bring a couple friends down here? They are pretty smart and might be able to help me a bit."

"Sure, sure, just make sure you keep an eye on them too," Daniel said as he looked around the room. "This place is a fantastic find. Amazing things have come out of this very room. But I have a very strong feeling that this is only the tip of the iceberg. This could be the start of something greater then we know, maybe even greater then we can imagine. If you think about it, this room could be anything. That map on the wall says this place could even be called EDEN, like the mythical place Adam and Eve were first tempted by the devil. With all that we have seen the last few weeks anything is possible."

"Dad, you know you are a bit theatrical sometimes?" Indy said rolling his eyes. "You realize that this place could be something else right?"

Daniel turned to stare at his son. "Like what junior?"

"Well I have a few ideas but one of my favourite ones so far is a storeroom for a crazy hermit German scientist from World War II," Indy said affecting a weird German accent.

His dad laughed hard enough to start crying. Tears rolled down his face as he struggled to breathe.

"Da, you could be right," he said wiping away the tears.

EDEN 8 – BULLETPROOF

The Veyron pulled through the main gates at a slow pace and went around the front to the main doors. Both father and son were in great spirits as they made their way back to the castle. James was waiting for them when they pulled up. Joslyn was there too, sitting on the edge of the fountain. She looked a little nervous as they got out of the car.

"Sirs," James said. "We have a situation. Zeus is in the op room on the monitors with Sasser. He is reporting a US naval destroyer parked just off the coast."

"No!" Daniel yelled. "We need more time, we're not ready yet."

Daniel was running up the stairs in the blink of an eye, the rest of them following fast on his heels.

"Joslyn," Indy said. "Go tell Jon what's going on make sure you guys stay inside."

He followed his dad and James up to the security operations room.

The security operations room was a buzz of activity. There were monitors on ever wall and smaller ones among control panels and tech equipment. Indy could see images from around the valley flicking on one of the larger sets. He saw everything in the valley there. The entire area had been blanketed in a security net. Every inch was monitored by a camera if not two.

On the main screen, a large grey ship sat idle in the water. The resolution was so good Indy could make out the sailors running back and forth on the deck.

"Bad news boss," Zeus said as they came in., "It looks like they are sending a team in. It will most likely be two gunships and two troop carriers. I'm guessing we might see a pair of SEAL teams on the ground. Oh, and if they are really serious they might send in a Tomahawk to soften us up."

"Ok Zeus I get it. We are in trouble. Sound the general quarter's sirens and call the security teams back to base. We don't need any one getting hurt. Make sure they know not to resist if they run into any soldiers," Daniel commanded as he looked at the displays.

"Sure thing boss," Zeus flipped a switch and then spoke into a microphone. "All teams back to base. Repeat back to base. Code red. Code red."

A siren started to wail in the distance. Metal shudders rolled down to cover the stained glass windows. Deep booms sounded through the entire castle.

Daniel watched the expression of awe on his son's face. "Those metal shutters were originally meant for tropical storm protection, they won't keep anyone out for long."

The intercoms blared with warnings. Attention attention. This is not a drill. Take immediate shelter. Repeat. This is not a drill.

"Look!" Indy was pointing at one of the smaller monitors. It was broadcasting snow. A second ago, he had been looking at the main road to Appleton.

"They're starting," Zeus said.

Several other monitors went dark.

"Looks like all non-shielded or Wi-Fi signals are down. Some cut but most likely jammed," Sasser said as his fingers danced over the controls. "Oh my god."

They all looked at the main display. A smoke trail had appeared from the destroyer.

"It's a cruise missile, tomahawk I think," Zeus said peering at the screens.

"Switching cameras to the long range castle turret," Sasser said quickly.

They could see a line of smoke low on the horizon.

Sasser gave them a countdown. "Impact to aurora in 3, 2, 1."

The missile bucked and seemed to hang in the air for a moment as the flame guttered and died. It still had enough momentum to continue past the aurora by several hundred feet. It crashed into a stand of trees and exploded in a brilliant flash that blinded the camera for a moment.

"Cool," Indy breathed out.

"No it was lucky," Sasser said. "I think the aurora interrupted its telemetry. Instead of hitting those trees, that missile could have hit this castle. Look at the Appleton road. The aurora is doing the same thing to the choppers. Looks like it even dropped one."

Zeus leaned over Sasser and swivelled the long-range camera around to look at the Appleton road barricade. It was a smoking ruin. They could see a pillar of smoke rising into the sky.

"Can't you get a better view Zeus?" demanded Daniel. "Zoom in or something."

"Ok. Let me try," Zeus fiddled with the long-range controls. He played with a couple of dials and the camera panned left and right before zooming in. "There we go."

They could see two attack choppers hovering in the distance and a larger transport helicopter sitting on the road. Another chopper was sitting on top of the barricade, smoke pouring from its engines. Soldiers were running back to the waiting line of choppers.

Something caught the sun in a quick rainbow.

"Oh no," Indy said in a whisper. "There are two statues on the road."

The soldiers had just made it across the red line. They kept running and finally made it to the choppers.

"Those soldiers didn't turn!" Sasser grunted and turned the main screen to the Appleton camera.

"Maybe they weren't inside long enough," Daniel said thoughtfully. "So those two statues... I think they might be our barricade team."

The military choppers lifted and banked away from the ruins of the barricade.

"Guess they've had enough," Zeus said. "Communications back online yet?"

"Negative," Sasser replied. We are still dark."

The door to the op room banged open just then and two metal canisters rolled in to the room.

Seconds later the room erupted with light and sound. Everyone dropped to the floor dazed and deaf. Everyone that is, except Indy. When the grenades rolled in, he saw them explode. He watched as the room brightened but it never got bright enough to blind him. He heard the metal cans rolling and pop but the noise didn't even ring his ears.

He had turned toward the door in time to see three men enter the room dressed in military gear. Each one was armed with a machine gun and the man on point snapped off a shot of at Indy's chest.

Time seemed to slow as he watched the muzzle flash and the black blur of the bullet. The bullet hit him center mass but it was like being hit with a pillow. It served only to push him into action. He moved two steps toward the man before several more bullets whizzed toward him, a couple of them missing his head by inches. With two more steps, Indy was among them. He barrelled into two of them and they crashed back out into the hall in a tumble.

Several flashes came from the room behind him as he fought with the men below him. It wasn't like the movies and it wasn't like training with his uncle. It wasn't elegant... it was chaos. Arms and legs came at him, a knife blade brushed across his cheek and deflected away. Indy rained heavy blows around him but wasn't sure if he was connecting with anything in the confusion. He was pulled off the pile by a large hand. Zeus picked him up from the pile and set him down lightly beside him.

"Whoa killer. I think they've had enough. You're lucky they weren't trying to kill you. I heard the shots," Zeus said as he smacked Indy's shoulder.

Indy looked down at the two soldiers at his feet. Both were bleeding heavily and both were unconscious.

"Indy are you ok?" His dad had come running from the other room and grabbed him in a fierce hug. "I heard the shots, are you hit?"

"I'm ok dad. I'm ok. What happened in there?"

"Well you remember how I told you my little friend was protective. Well look..." Daniel said motioning Indy to look into the ops room.

Inside the room there was an unconscious soldier and a little panda monk sitting on top of his chest. The soldier groaned once and the monk kicked him hard in the temple.

"Nice work little dude. Joslyn would just love you..."

"Joslyn! Jon!" Indy yelled suddenly remembering his friends downstairs.

Indy ran for the entertainment room, footsteps thumping after him. He knew it was too late before he even got into the room. The couch was overturned and the room's French doors were broken inward. The metal door covering the balcony had been breached. He found Jon under the overturned couch with two small burns on his neck, he was still breathing and looked to be uninjured. Joslyn was nowhere to be found.

James ran into the room behind him, running past Indy and to the broken doors. "They came in this way. Look they left their climbing ropes."

Indy ran out onto the balcony behind James. Together they scanned the landscape.

"There! I see a boat on the beach." James was pointing down the cliffs at the beach below. "They must be taking her there."

Sure enough Indy could make out two dark figures just beginning to rappel down towards their boat. He was sure one of them had a body slung over his shoulder.

James checked his earpiece. "Radios are still out. Wait here, I'll go get help." James was out of the room in a flash.

"I can't wait for them James," Indy thought aloud. "They won't get there in time."

Without looking, Indy took a flying leap over the balcony rail. He landed hard but was up on his feet and running within seconds.

Before long he was looking over the cliffs edge, staring down as the soldiers reached the beach at the bottom. They were making their way across the expanse of sand toward a small boat.

Indy looked down at the repelling ropes. He had never climbed one before and had no idea where to start. Besides, he knew it would take him too long to get down to the beach. Looking down again at the beach his vertigo assailed him.

He took two quick steps back from the edge and closed his eyes. He started to breathe again as he tried to calm down. Bullets couldn't hurt him, knives couldn't scratch him and pillows... well he still felt pillows. A smile crossed his face as he recalled Joslyn slamming him with that pillow. Just the thought of her sobered his thoughts and cleared his mind. They were almost to the boat now. It was now or never. He started towards the cliff.

His nerves failed him again as he shuddered to a stop at the edge.

"I can do this," he said to the wind.

He took a deep breath and jumped. He was bulletproof but he was no superman. Indy fell like a rock and started to overbalance halfway down. His arms pin wheeled as he attempted to try to correct his flight but he ended up head first and tumbling. A scream must have torn from his lips because the men on the beach looked up at him as he fell.

The sandy beach below rushed up at him faster than he could believe. He ended up landing feet first by some incredible chance of fate. The sand exploded from his landing site like a cannonball hitting water. When he opened his eyes, Indy was laying on his belly staring at the sides of a small crater of sand. He quickly looked over the top of the sand and saw one of the soldiers coming toward him.

Indy crawled from his sand pit and stood tall on the beach. "Let her go!" he screamed.

The words had only just cleared his lips when the soldier shot him.

One, two, three shots all hit Indy in the chest. It did not even faze him this time. After taking a few running strides at the soldier he heard a pfumppp sound and the next thing he knew something exploded behind him. Indy was catapulted forward, flying towards the soldier.

When he stood up again he was only feet from the soldier, he could even see the SEAL TEAM insignia stitched into the soldiers uniform. Indy just grinned at the SEAL as he started toward him again.

You have to give the man credit, there was no shocked look of terror, no scream of impending doom. He simply called to the other man waiting in the boat. "Go, go, go." With that, the man pulled a large nasty looking knife from his belt. The soldier crouched and motioned Indy forward.

Indy ran at him hard and jumped at the man like a linebacker. The man was laughing... Laughing! At Indy as he sailed by the sidestepping soldier. Indy brushed by the man and then thudded hard face first into the sand. When he shifted his arms under his body, he paused just a moment before rising.

Before he could get to his feet, he felt a hard pressure at the base of his skull and a knee thudded into his back.

Indy was pinned to the sand with his arms still under his chest. He tried to roll but the bigger man was just too strong.

"Let her go!" Indy screamed into the sand.

Words whispered in his ear. "Look kid... I'm really sorry but I can't. I have my orders and now your gonna have to come too." The soldier grabbed for his wrists and within seconds, Indy was bound hand and foot. Then his body was thrown over the man's shoulder like a bag of flour.

The soldier in the rowboat had come back to the beach and together they tossed Indy into the bottom of the boat. Joslyn's body was limp beside him as the two soldiers looked down at him.

One of the SEALs looked at his watch. "He's past due."

"Yup. Let's head out."

A sharp whistle brought both of their heads and guns around as a third SEAL came running up the beach.

"Just in time, Commander."

"Stow this." A harsh voice spoke as a large rucksack landed in the boat followed by an older grizzly bear of a man. "Move out," The commander said.

"Sir, yes sir," both soldiers said in unison.

Indy knew there wasn't much time to act. He had to find a way out of the boat before it got to the aurora's barrier. An idea came to him as checked his shirt and felt for the object he had hidden there. It was stroke of pure luck that his hands were tied in front of his chest. He just needed to wait until they were in deeper water so his plan would work.

The Commander glared down at Indy. "Just keep your mouth shut kid and everything will be fine. We are taking you two back to the ship. We have a medical staff on standby and if the doctors clear you then... You'll both be returned to your homes."

A whisper from behind the commander caused a look of frustration to cross the man's grizzly face.

Indy caught a small part of the whisper "...freak," someone said.

"What can it do?" the Commander asked as his look soured.

"Not sure. I hit him with three rounds and there's not a mark on him. It didn't even slow him down."

"Great, looks like we can add another fricken statue to the collection. What about the girl?" the Commander asked.

The first soldier in the boat hesitated before answering. "She's ok, she screamed a bit but got real quiet when we Tazed her."

"Well if we can salvage one good thing out of this cluster duck I will be amazed. At least Bravo team did their job." The Commander looked around the boat for the knapsack.

The Commander nudged the bag that lay beside Indy's head. "I was able to secure a few of the artifacts from the power plant. These little things are gonna make the geek squad giddy."

The rucksack beside him shifted again and Indy could hear something clinking in the bag but couldn't get a good look at it.

They rowed into the surf with the waves tossing the little zodiac boat up and down. The rucksack banged into him several times before Indy got an idea.

The next time the bag came close to his face, Indy sank his teeth into its tie cord. As the bag fell back away from him, Indy whipped his head around the opposite way.

The bag came untied and on the next wave began spilling some of its contents around the floor of the boat. Small pop can sized crystal orbs bounced and rolled between him and Joslyn.

The rowing stopped as the Commander yelled, "God dam it McCoy! Don't you know how to stow your gear, get those things back in the bag. Stop! Don't touch them with your bare hand."

The soldiers around them whipped off jackets or shirts and chased the crystal balls around the bottom of the boat.

Indy was straining at his bindings when a globe came bouncing back at him. At the last second, the orb was deflected away by a combat boot.

The crystal ball instead struck Joslyn in the forehead. It hit her hard enough to leave a little gash that seeped a bit of blood. The orb seemed to light up with a spark as it rolled away. Joslyn's eyes flew open and focused on Indy lying on the boat beside her.

"Indy? Where are we?" she asked in a daze.

"The military stormed the castle," he said. "I think they are after the crystals. I ripped open a bag of them just before you woke up. We are in the water now, probably pretty close to the aurora."

She nodded keeping her eyes on him. Her bright blue eyes still looked a little dazed.

"I've got a plan... Can you swim?" Indy said in a whisper.

She whispered her reply, "Yes."

"Ok when I tell you, try to roll over the side and get into the water. Try to get back to the beach if you can."

"What are you going to do?" she tried to ask but Indy was already moving.

He grabbed for the grenade he had stolen from the soldier during his fight on the beach. He tugged on his shirt and pulled the grenade out.

"Now," Indy said loudly.

He pulled the grenade's pin with his teeth and rolled away from Joslyn placing his body between her and the grenade.

He waited until he heard a splash from behind him before releasing the grenades catch.

He closed his eyes and waited.

"Please let this work," he prayed as the moments ticked by in his head.

The explosion blew the little zodiac out of the water. Debris flew among flying bodies. Indy was tossed up in the air like a ragdoll. He came down in the water, hands, and feet still bound together.

The water pulled him down deep into its depths. Without his arms and legs free, he was sinking like a stone. Panic was overriding his senses and before he realized it, his mouth was full of seawater.

The salty water was rushing into his body but somehow it wasn't affecting his breathing. The moment of panic soon passed and Indy relaxed as he realized he could still breathe. The water flowed into his mouth and down his throat. It filled his lungs and then flowing back out again just as easy. Indy looked around as he came to rest on the sandy ocean floor.

The water was dark and he couldn't see more than a few feet in either direction. Several fish swam past investigating his presence in their territory. It was calm and peaceful sitting there in silence, he could have sat there for hours.

But he needed to check on Joslyn, he had to make sure she was safe and get her back to the beach. Something in his gut told him she was still in trouble. With an effort, he kicked off the sandy bottom and dolphin kicked his way back to the surface.

The ocean current was pulling him out to sea as he came to the surface of the water. He was able to bob on the surface but being bound left him unable to make any real headway against the relentless surf.

Behind him, the soldiers were clinging to the sides of the wrecked zodiac their quick reflexes saving them from the brunt of the blast. They had already started making their own way out to sea dragging the boat along with them.

A buoy that he hadn't noticed before bobbed just feet from the aurora close to where he was just barely treading water. There was nothing else in sight. He was still drifting towards the buoy when he heard a soft moaning. It was coming from the other side of the buoy. Hope flared in his eyes and he started to angle towards the bobbing marker.

Bubbles erupted in the water around him as he entered the shimmering lights of the aurora. His entire body instantly began to feel energized almost as if an electric current was passing through him. Something tugged at his legs from under the water and the bonds binding his legs broke. A second later Indy could feel some more tugging around his hands. An instant later, he was free.

With his arms and legs free, it only took several long strokes to bring him close to the buoy. Before he got there, his skin started to tingle. A coldness crept into his muscles and he almost stopped. Then he heard a desperate voice cry out. "Help me!"

It was Joslyn! He could see her holding onto the far edge of the large metal buoy.

"Don't worry I've gotcha," he said as he swam closer.

"No Indy... stay, there," she said. "The buoy is... drifting in and out of the... I'll come to you. But I don't think... I can't swim like this," she held up one hand. It was crystalized and gleaming in the sunlight.

She kicked off the buoy and swam weakly to him. He held her in his arms for a moment and hugged her tight. One side of her face was covered in frost and her left eye had turned a milky blue.

"Don't worry I've got you," he soothed.

He put an arm around her waist and had her float on her back. He started dragging her back to shore as the waves pushed them towards the beach.

"I've got you," he continued to say as he brought her back to safety.

EDEN 9 – FROST SCARS

The next morning Daniel Locke called a formal meeting and requested everyone living inside the valley attend. He had asked everyone attend and every single person came as requested. There were a few notable exceptions, the three SEALs they had captured last night were secured somewhere at the hydro station. Zeus and James were down there on guard duty. Hank had stayed put at his place because he really didn't feel up to coming. Two other people were missing as well. Indy could hear the murmured talk about the two missing men from the Appleton barricade. Their bodies were still visible by the long-range cameras in the main tower. Their crystalized statues lay just feet beyond the aurora.

Today the great room was packed. Long tables had been set out with benches for seating. More people stood at the sides of the room. A stage was setup at the front of the room and a large glass podium stood empty and waiting for a speaker.

Doc Hocking had just finished a presentation about his latest findings. His conclusion was that the aurora's size and electrical charge were stable and constant. He could not foresee the aurora expanding into the neighbouring town of Appleton or shrinking in upon itself. However, without more knowledge of the technology behind the aurora it was impossible to say how long it would last. His best guess on its possible duration based on his findings would be years if not longer.

Indy sat with Joslyn and Jon among the crowd. Joslyn was wearing a hoody pulled up to cover her face and a pair of soft leather gloves to hide her frosted hand. The room was loud and uneasy as they waited for his father's announcement.

When Daniel Locke walked onto the stage from the backroom, he was greeted with quiet applause. He was dressed in his finest suit and was carrying the white staff. The audience hushed as he approached the podium.

"Thank you all for coming," he said gravely. "I guess the best way to deal with this situation is to break it down piece by piece."

"As you know currently our little valley is under military quarantine. No one is or will be allowed to enter or leave this valley. All communication with the outside world has also been severed by the military as of last night. We are completely on our own for the time being."

The audience broke out in chattering.

"Please quiet down," Daniel said as he held his hands up.

"As you know yesterday the United States sent an attack force against us in an attempt to secure technology vital to national security. During the attack, two of our security team, Sean O'dede and Lawrence Punch, were forcibly taken outside the aurora. Both of these people were crystalized around five feet from the edge of the aurora. We have also discovered some distressing news. As some of you have already heard, re-entering the aurora has been found to be… unhealthy. When a crystalized living organism re-enters the aurora the solid crystal melts away but leaves a sort of perma-frost tissue in its place. It would be easiest to compare this process to frostbite. Skin and other tissue changes and no longer resembles normal healthy living tissue. We are referring to that symptom as a frost scar. The frost scar is not diminished by water or body heat and it appears that internal organs may be permanently damaged. In other words for your safety please do not attempt to pass through the aurora at this time, even for a moment."

"In addition to the barricade assault there were several minor skirmishes that were fought in and around the castle and several people were injured. Due to some quick thinking by our security team none of those people lost their lives."

He stopped and looked into the crowd until he found his son's eyes.

"We are not quite sure why this happened but a few of my advisors suggest that it was a fact finding mission or a pre-emptive strike," Daniel took a deep breath before continuing. "It may possibly be an overreaction to our implied advanced technology."

"Before you ask the answer is no," Daniel said. "We have no advanced weaponry. Doc is working hard to identify several unknown artifacts but so far none of the artifacts we have found could be considered weaponized."

"In other words we are on our own. I have had a long conversation with the President of the USA. He has given me his word that the U.S. will not send any more personnel into the area. We have an understanding that the SEALs we have under guard will remain our guests until they can be assured safe passage through the aurora."

Quite a few of the audience grumbled at this news. Indy was sure that given a choice the more vocal members of the room would see the SEALs thrown out of the aurora beside their friends at the barricade.

Daniel cleared his throat as the murmurs subsided. "The President has also agreed to declare the aurora a new temporary border. For the time being, nothing will be allowed to pass in or out of that border. This decision has become law and will be enforced by a United Nations task force."

The crowd went absolutely silent. Not a single person moved, spoke, or even breathed for ten heartbeats.

Daniel continued his speech as the shocked audience broke out in chatter. "The President had no other choice in this matter. Global pressure by several powerful countries has made this a necessary step for worldwide stability. The fear is that the artifacts found in our valley could be used as the basis of a new arms race. Countries such as China and Russia fear that the United States will seize this technology for itself and upset the balance of current world peace."

"The President assured me that these measures are only temporary. But... they need to be enforced unilaterally to ensure world peace. He is meeting daily with the United Nations to seek a better solution for us all. Unfortunately that means we will have absolutely no contact with anyone outside this valley for the time being."

"Life at this castle and the surrounding area will be much harder without outside support, but not impossible. With hard work, we can become totally self-sufficient. We have all the tools, equipment, and knowledge we need to make a great life for us all. We don't know how long the aurora will separate us from the outside world but in the meantime I assure you we can and will prosper here."

EDEN 10 – HERE COMES THE BOOM

Doc Hocking stormed through the door of his lab at the hydro plant. It was still a wreck from the SEAL attack but he would not let anyone else in to clean it.

"Fools! Idiots!" he yelled and kicked at several tables that had been overturned.

The animal cages were empty as well, the cage doors broken and hanging loose. The animals that were inside the cages were now scattered into the surrounding woods.

He went to his hidden alcove and slid it open. Racks and racks of egg crystals lined the cabinet in rows. All of his free time of late had gone into experimenting with the little black box. With just a little bit of searching through different images he had found DNA strands of many exotic creatures and even some extinct ones. By experimentation, he had created creatures of legend and myth. Humans with pale gold skin and long ears he called Elves. A jack rabbit crossed with an antelope gave him the curious Jackelope. He had even found a sub setting that clothed the creatures in outfits of many odd designs.

It was frustrating to find he could not hatch any one of them. Unlike Daniel Locke's companion panda bear, his creations were locked solidly in their crystal prison. He had spent hours trying to free the beasts before he finally confronted Daniel about his creature. The man had lied straight to his face. He didn't hatch the creature... it just magically appeared to him. Bull. Such an obvious lie, the man probably had a half dozen others secreted around the castle.

Doc ran his fingers casually across the surfaces of several eggs until he came to his favourite. He had created it by combining the DNA from his own blood with that of a black bull. The figure was quite an impressive sight. It had a bull's head and massive muscular shoulders, a sleek body and human legs. Chain mail shorts and a thick leather belt completed its unique look. It was a Minotaur straight from Greek mythology. Its face had a bit more human look to it than others he had seen in the movies, but it was beautiful. He slipped the egg into his chest pocket and slid closed his secret door.

As the door slid shut, it clicked into place. The doctor stood staring at the door trying to puzzle out something in his head. The click... it hadn't done that before. The doctor turned from the cabinet and took a few small steps before an explosion ripped through the room.

EDEN 11 – GOT HAM?

The castle was buzzing with talk of the explosion at the hydro plant. No one knew if the explosion had been an accident or an artifact experiment gone wrong. Luckily, there had only been one injury, Doc Hocking.

The doctor had been severely injured in the blast. To his great fortune, Jolie Locke had been touring the experiments room at that exact time. With the help of a few fellow scientists, she had braved the destruction and fires to bring her healing staff to the rescue. Most people agreed that without her help the good doctor would have surely perished. Neither the doctor's lab nor any of the artifacts stored within survived the explosion. Rescuers had relayed news of the destruction and the broken pieces of crystal that were strewn around the room.

The devastation was so extensive that a large hole was blown through the wall of the building housing the lab.

Indy and Joslyn walked into his dad's office in the tallest tower as James stormed out. The man was in such a hurry he didn't even bother saying hi to the kids on the way past. Daniel Locke was sitting behind a stately wooden desk with his head bowed low. He looked up as they entered the room and a smile quickly spread across his face.

"Hey kids, what can I do for you two?" he asked.

"Dad, Joslyn's got an idea," Indy said. "Go ahead and tell him Joslyn."

Joslyn nodded and started her story. "Well... back when I was younger my dad had a hobby," Joslyn said in a quiet reserved voice. "He had this old radio equipment, a ham radio. Anyway I remember one day playing with the dials and picking up some people speaking Japanese."

"My dad told me I had managed to bounce the signal off the atmosphere because of some low cloud cover. Anyway I was able to listen to them talk for a little while. My dad said that we could have spoken with them if we could talk Japanese."

"How does this help us?" Daniel said a bit irritated. "We don't have any old equipment like that around here."

"I know someone who might," Joslyn said unperturbed. "Back then my dad was part of a chain of ham operators. He had a few friends that he talked to in the winter months when no one really wanted to leave their homes. One of them was Hank Abbott."

"Really? Our apple-loving farmer? I wonder if that old man still has his gear," Daniel paused as he considered his options. "Why don't you two head down to the orchard and have a chat with Hank."

"Can we take the Veyron?" Indy begged excitedly.

His dad looked at him more pointedly.

"Ah. Ok. How about the-"

"You can take the jeep," Daniel said with a small smile touching his lips. "I had it specially built for you as a welcome home present. With all the stuff going on I had forgotten about it until now."

Indy smiled widely. "Thanks dad, you're the best."

Daniel waved at the pair and went back to shuffling papers. Indy grabbed Joslyn's hand and together they raced down to the garage. They ran into Jon and Allen in the halls on their way.

"You guys want to go for a little ride?" Indy asked, his excitement contagious.

Allen declined the invite because he had to make a few deliveries but Jon agreed to come in a heartbeat.

When the three kids walked into the garage, they saw the big jeep shining in one corner of the room. The jeep must have been covered up the last time he came through because Indy didn't remember seeing it before.

"That thing is a monster!" Jon said.

The jeep was large, shiny, and red. Huge tires lifted it high into the air. Deep black roll bars and grill guards framed the beast. Large spotlights filled almost every open spot on the light bar. It was beautiful and it was all his.

Indy looked at his friends as they stood in awe of the jeep.

He also noticed it was the first time in days Joslyn was smiling.

"Wanna drive?" he asked Joslyn as he hopped into the shotgun seat.

"Really?" she asked.

Jon looked a bit disappointed but hopped into the back seat without a word. Indy hoped that he understood that she needed a little bit of cheering up.

The jeep started with a deep throaty growl and within minutes, they were bouncing down the road. They took several off road short cuts on their way to Hanks, each one muddier then the last. The jeep just soaked it all up, mud, and bumps, ruts and rocks. Joslyn's left eye might have been frost scarred but it didn't slow down her driving skills in the least.

By the time, they got to Hanks Store the red jeep was a solid mass of moving mud. Joslyn pulled into the parking lot in a cloud of dust and mud. The parking lot at Hanks was empty except for the old man's battered old pickup. The sinkhole was still barricaded in one far corner of the lot. They could see Hank on the porch in his favourite chair, his dog Snoop by his side. The old man waved as they pulled in.

"Hey Hank, Hey Snoop," they called.

The dog barked happily and jumped on Jon.

"Hey kids what brings you folks down to my little orchard?" Hank said from the porch.

"Dad wanted me to see if you had a ham radio," Indy said. "Joslyn was telling us we might be able to bounce a signal past the jammers and get a message out."

"Hmmm," Hank drawled. "Not sure if it will work but I might have it in the attic. If I do it's gonna take some time to get out and running. Let me set you kids up with some pie and cider and then I'll go see what I can find."

Cider was poured into thick glass masonry jars and slices of pie were scooped onto plates. Within a few minutes, they were sitting out back on Hanks picnic table enjoying the weather and food.

They finished there pies quickly and Jon volunteered to run the plates and mugs back inside.

Indy and Joslyn sat silently side by side in the sunlight. Joslyn's hand was uncovered and glistening in the sun.

Indy's hand casually brushed against her frosted bare hand. "Does it hurt?" he asked.

"No," she said as she turned away slightly but he held her shoulders.

"Don't," she said softy. "I'm ugly now, I'm a freak and half blind."

"You're not a freak," Indy said. "You are beautiful."

He brushed the frost on the side of her face as it sparkled in the sun. The stands of crystal hair framed her face. She was beautiful, the changes only made her more so in his eyes.

They closed their eyes and leaned into each other to kiss.

Their lips had touched for only a second when Joslyn's eyes popped open and she fell back.

"Nooo!" she cried.

She had her eyes closed and her head pointed at him.

"Huh?" Indy asked confused. "What are you talking about?"

"When I closed my eyes I saw you. But..." she stuttered. "There were these shadows all over you, it looked like you were being eaten."

Her head swivelled around the clearing with her eyes closed. "It's all changed. The air is alive with, something. Like dust motes in sunlight, but they move like bees."

"Can you still see them?" Indy said putting an arm around her shoulders to try and calm her.

She looked at him again then closed her eyes.

"No," she said. "I can't see anything now."

Indy spotted two people coming around the store. "Here comes Jon and Hank now, just try to relax. It was probably nothing but we can have the Doc check out your eye when we get back."

Joslyn didn't look convinced and anything but relaxed but she did take a deep shuddering breath.

Hank was beaming with pride as they walked up to the picnic table.

"I got it working with big Jon's help," Hank said with a huge grin on his face. "It's just warming up in the shop."

The big farmer led them back into the shop to a table and chair. The old radio equipment sitting on the table was buzzing with energy.

"You remember how to work it Little Cloud?" Hank asked Joslyn.

Joslyn blushed at her childhood radio nickname.

"Roger that Apple Maker," she said as she sat down.

Hank dipped his head and smiled.

They dialled the equipment in and started listening. Occasional one of them would grab the microphone and try to broadcast but they weren't able to get anything but squelch out of the old rig.

Then a squabble came through the speakers.

"Copy that Big Ben. Over and out," a voice with a British accent said.

Joslyn and Hank grabbed for the microphone at the same time. But by the time they keyed in the microphone the signal was gone.

"Well, at least we know it works," Jon said grinning at the two dejected radio operators.

Joslyn slammed the microphone down and covered her eyes with her hands.

She sobbed quietly for a bit before raising her head. "I can't handle this, this stuff. I want to go home. I miss my family."

Hanks big paw of a hand came down softly on her shoulder. "I know Little Cloud," he said. "Sometimes life throws curve balls. I know from experience. A big part of me has been missing since I lost my Mags. Maggie was my love and life. I lost my soul mate over ten years ago. For a long time I was just treading water and just barely keeping it together."

"How do you go on?" Joslyn asked as tears glistened from her right eye.

"It's not about going on. It's about rebuilding. Relearning in some cases and it's not easy," Hank looked to Indy and Jon. "Sometimes you dwell on the bad things so much you forget the good things you still have."

"You know this whole mess could be over tomorrow and we could all be back to normal," Jon said, trying to comfort her.

Indy tried his luck. "Have some faith Joslyn. We are in the middle of something incredible. I think we should go have a look at the room my dad found. Maybe we could find something they missed."

"We can take turns on the radio scanning for signals," Jon volunteered. "Hank you mind going first? We will be back in a bit."

EDEN 12 – THE SWORD AND THE STICKS

They took the hidden stairs down into a small underground tunnel that led into the large vaulted room. Someone had installed lights and hung them high on the walls, bathing the room in a warm white light. Thick extension cables ran back up the stairs into Hanks shop above. As they walked around the room, Joslyn began tracing swirls and patterns that were carved deep into the stone. Jon was thumping the hard stone walls and floor trying to gauge the stones thickness.

"This place is empty," he said sourly. "Not even a hidden wall or trapdoor. Just a bunch of old Latin scribbles."

There wasn't a speck of dust on any surface in the room and the room had long since been cleaned out of anything that could be removed.

"Look at this," Joslyn was standing at the center of the room looking down with her eyes closed. "Indy? Jon? Do you see the writing? It's all over the walls. It's beautiful… all wavy and filled with leaves, vines, and flowers."

Indy looked around at the walls ceiling and floor. "I don't see anything," he paused for a moment as another headache blossomed behind his eyes. They had been coming a lot more frequently as of late. He closed his eyes and tried to relax.

Jon's voice brought him out of his daze. "You can read Latin Joslyn? I'm impressed. I can only read a bit of it myself."

Joslyn walked to one side and started to trace the wall again. This time with her eyes closed.

"No, this isn't Latin," she whispered. "It's in English. There seems to be one centerline running around the whole room. Valhalla, Mount Olympus, Atlantis, Hades, Heaven... Look here's Eden again," she giggled. "It's even got a little gold apple above it."

"Really?" Indy was curious now and he walked over to where she said the apple was. He ran his fingers over the spot she was pointing at.

A frown appeared on Joslyn's face. "The apples gone now."

She spun to look at the room. "It's over there now, can you see it? It's on the floor over there."

Jon stood in the center of the room looking down at the floor.

Indy turned to look, lifting his hand from the wall as he did.

"Great now that one's gone too," she huffed. "I wonder what they are."

Indy's hand descended on the wall again, trying to find the apple Joslyn described.

"It's back again, right under your feet Jon," Joslyn said quickly.

Jon bent down and brushed his fingers on the floor under his feet and this time a hissing started. The sound came from the far corner of the room.

Part of the floor across from them started to drop away. A deep blue glow surged around the stone edges. When they walked over to the hole, they could see steep stairs leading down.

Indy scanned the room and noticed one other thing had changed.

The stairs leading up to Hanks store were gone, covered over by a newly appeared section of wall. Indy ran over to where the doorway had been and pounded hard. "Hank! Hank!"

"It's no use that wall is too thick. I can't hear anything but my hands hitting the stone. At least the lights are still working, I am surprised that the cables weren't severed," Indy said.

Joslyn looked at her friends and motioned them to follow. "So down it is then. I guess opportunity just came knocking."

Indy laughed. "Ok but let me lead. If there's anything down there, chances are it can't hurt me."

"Oh, my hero," she teased and batted her eyelashes.

"Cut it out. Let's get going," Jon said as he shoved Indy into the lead.

The stairs curved down to follow the walls gentle curve. It dropped down over fifteen feet to the floor of the next level.

They made their way down and stopped on the last step. The room was dark and silent.

"See anything Joslyn?" Indy asked over his shoulder.

"Nothing," she said. "Wait...nope, just your big head," she laughed. "Would you hurry it up and get down there. The lights are starting to glow. I can see vines and patterns again."

"Any apples?" Jon asked.

"Nope," Joslyn said as she peered around. "Nothing else is lighting up but I can see dark shapes all over the room."

"Ok, let's look around real quick and if we can't find anything we can go back and wait for help by the sinkhole," Indy said, as he made ready to leave the stairs.

They didn't have to worry about the lights. As soon as Indy's foot touched the floor, electricity filled the air. The vines Joslyn had been talking about lit around them like a fuse. The light from the vines spread through the room lighting ever surface with brilliant light.

This time, they all could see the lights. Around them, the room was full of random things, armoured dummies, racks of swords and other martial weapons. Small statuettes and chests were scattered over several tables and shelves. The biggest thing in the room was a large box at the center of the room.

The box was wrapped in the same pulsing stone vines as the rest of the room. One golden apple was carved into the top of the box.

Indy walked over to it and looked around it. He put his hands on it and shoved. It didn't even budge. "It looks like it is part of the floor. The vines in the floor continue up the sides of the box and then back down again."

They all walked over to stand beside the vine-covered box, Joslyn with eyes closed and Indy with his eyes open. They were all transfixed by the large carved box.

Jon ran his hand around the edge of the box. "I don't see any hinges or holes... wait a sec."

Jon had just traced the outside edge of the apple when the box shuddered then the room flashed as if someone had just taken a picture.

The apple lit with a golden light and the box lid lifted on its own. They peered into the box.

It was empty.

They spent the next few hours poking at the artifacts on the tables and admiring the fine armour on the stands. One armour set was small enough for Joslyn but the rest of it was meant for people much bigger than Indy.

Jon went right to the long swords. He picked up the largest and swung it around. It hummed in the air with an audible energy.

"This thing is so light," he marvelled.

Joslyn tried on the small armour set. The pieces slid into each other and sealed without any visible straps. Each piece fit like it had been made for her. There were wings on the helm and angels on her shoulders. A slinky soft under garment covered the gaps between each piece.

She caught the boys gawking at her.

"What are you looking at punks?" she admonished but smiled as she turned away from them.

Indy just smiled and turned away himself. He walked over to the sword rack and picked up the first sword he saw.

He noticed his dragon tattoo just then. The little black dragon was wrapped around his wrist and across the back of his hand. It was shaking its head at the weapon in his grasp. The black dragon seemed to shift slightly on his hand and Indy felt a tugging at his wrist. On a hunch, Indy put down the sword and moved his hand down the row of weapons. At each weapon, the dragon shook its head. The last weapons in the rack were a pair of three-foot long rods. Each one was carved with tiny dragons. The dragon nodded once and disappeared back up his arm.

The sticks were like feathers in his hands when he lifted them. They seemed to vibrate in his hands.

As he spun around, he saw Joslyn had come over and was pulling free a small sword that matched the angels on her shoulders. Wings formed the cross guard and a pair of angels flew the length of the blade.

"Engarde!" Joslyn had a wide smile on her face as she waved the slim bladed sword at him.

"Ok you asked for it lady," he growled.

"Bring it punk," she grunted.

They made slow clumsy swings at each other. Several of the swings missing the other person's weapon completely. They laughed and danced around the room like drunken pirates. After a few minutes, they gained a rhythm.

Jon stood back and cheered for Joslyn.

Clack, clack, swing.

Clack, clack, swing.

Indy started to get fancy. He added spins and twirls after each pattern. In turn, Joslyn began to get in on the game. The short sword had the greater reach and she used long sweeping strokes to keep him out of reach.

Somewhere during their game, it began to get serious. They had started to outdo each other. Then the swings started to get a little faster, then a little harder. The smiles and laughter turned to grunts and grimaces.

The game ended when one of Indy's sticks flashed down on an arm guard. There was a flash and the arm guard cracked. At the same time, Joslyn's blade came down on Indy's leg. Instead of a flash, a scream tore from his lips. He dropped to the ground clutching at his leg. There was no blood but the pain of the blow had shocked him. It was the strongest feeling he had since passing through the aurora.

"Are you all right?" Joslyn asked as she rushed over.

"Yea, no damage. I'm good," Indy said.

"Thank goodness," she smiled.

Indy's heart leapt in his chest at that smile and he notice the red blush on Joslyn's face grow as he returned the smile with his lopsided grin.

Jon was poking through some chests on the other side of the room. He had lost interest in their mock battle after several minutes of the clumsy fight. He had brought his head up only long enough to make sure they were all right after Indy's scream.

"Indy? Joslyn? Jon? Where are you guys?" A voice called to them from above.

"We're down here!" They all yelled at the same time.

Indy's parents swept down the stairs and into the room. James and Hank were not far behind.

EDEN 13 – HE SELLS EGG SHELLS

Indy snapped awake to the noise of a door closing somewhere down the hall. Looking around he saw that he was in his own apartment back at the castle. He didn't remember how he had gotten there last night. In fact, he didn't even remember what he was doing most of last night. Although he was sure it was just another night of movies and popcorn with Joslyn and Jon. He put a hand up to his head as a wave of dizziness and another headache set in. The room seemed to swirl and sway around him and he decided to stay in bed just a little longer. Images of the last couple of days flicked through his mind as he tried to relax. The little black dragon shaking his head, the SEALs bursting into the op room, diving off the cliff and then Joslyn's sad face filled his mind. Her sad blue eyes stared back at him. One eye turned a milky blue and the frost on her face shimmered in the sunlight. His breath caught in his throat as he remembered her frosted fingertips running down his cheek and across his lips. He wished he could feel her cold skin or even her warm breath on his cheek.

However, he could not because of the dragon. Whatever had saved his life on two occasions now prevented him from feeling her soft caress. As well as the burning impact of a grenade explosion, he thought to himself. He opened his eyes and watched silently as the dragon moved down his shoulder to his forearm. The sinewy black dragon entwined itself on his arm and gazed back at him. Its red eyes seemed to burn right into his soul. Indy could almost feel what it was thinking. Maybe he was just imagining it but in his mind, he heard. "There are many things in life that are not fair, but what really matters in life, is living."

The dragon had stopped moving and closed its eyes. Indy reached out to stroke the dragon with his other hand. If it was a trick of the mind or not Indy didn't know but he decided to try to communicate. Indy cleared his throat and said. "Whatever you are, you saved my life. I am grateful for that." The dragon's eye popped open and the creature smiled a toothy grin before the eye closed again.

Indy's head had stopped throbbing by now and he decided it was a good time to go and get some breakfast. He got dressed quickly and headed out into the hall.

He found the castle quiet and deserted until he got closer to the converted hospital wing. There was a figure in white ahead of him moving through the doors leading into the hospital wing. He knew it was his mom from the white staff in her hand and the short quick strides of her walk. Indy hurried to catch up.

"Hey mom!" Indy called as he finally caught up to her. "Wait up."

Jolie Locke turned with a brilliant smile and held her arms wide. "Indy." she said as they hugged. He loved it when she called him that. During his childhood, he had grown to despise being called junior. One day, when he was young, he had decided to pick a new name for himself. Indy was just another word for "independent" which was exactly what he was looking for. Indy was smiling to himself at the fond memory as his mother took him by the arm and led him down the hall.

"Your father has been looking for you," she said. "Where have you been all day?"

Indy shrugged not wanting to tell her about the blackout. "Just hanging out."

"Well your dad needs to see you. You can call him right after this," she said patting his arm as they walked. "How is your friend Joslyn doing? How is she handling the whole frost scar issue?"

Indy looked sideways at his mom. He was sure she was digging for something more than just how his friend was doing. His mom had a way of finding out even the smallest details of his life. So naturally, he deflected.

"She was pretty scared about the whole abduction thing a lot more, but at least she's alive."

"You were very brave going after her like that," Jolie said. "Stupid but brave. You are just lucky those soldiers were ordered to capture, not kill. I can't even begin to think…" Jolie's eyes began to tear up.

He had avoided telling anyone about the dragon and being bulletproof. Luckily, no one had seen any of the incidents happen. Flash bang grenades had blinded everyone in the security room and the gunshots were being described as warning shots. On the water against the SEALs, it had only been Indy and Joslyn. Both Joslyn and Jon knew his secret but had promised to keep it for him. The last thing he wanted was to become ones of Doc's lab rats. Besides, he liked the attention his parents lavished on him for being brave.

"I know you like her Indy," Jolie said with a grin. "But please try to be more careful in the future."

In retrospect, maybe he could have changed the topic a bit better. He couldn't help it that Joslyn was on his mind a lot lately.

They had reached the end of the hall and Jolie took a deep breath before pushing the door open and stepping through.

Inside Doc Hocking lay wrapped up like a mummy in a horror film. The Doc lay staring at the ceiling as they walked into the room.

"Hello doctor," Doc Hocking joked as they entered. "Doing the rounds again I see. Oh and this must be the new intern you have been talking about." The doctor started laughing at his own jokes but broke down in a fit of hacking and coughing.

"That doesn't sound so good Doc," Indy said. Turning to his mom, he asked. "How come you haven't healed him yet?"

"Well you see junior," the Doc sneered. "Sometimes things are a little more complicated then what you see at first glance." The old man reached across his chest and peeled back his bandages. Small crystal shards were imbedded deep in his skin, down the man's entire left side.

"It appears that the crystal shards I obtained in the explosion of my lab have granted me a partial resistance to your mother's gift. Although the little gems are slightly counterproductive to my health, the results are quite amazing. I think my little friend agrees with me as well." The doctor nodded towards a small Minotaur statuette on the table next to his bed. The half bull, half man statue was incredibly detailed with heavy sculpted muscles and a broad chest. Even its small beady eyes appeared to follow Indy around the room.

When Indy stepped closer to examine the statue, his mom put a hand on his shoulder. "Wait a moment," she commanded. Her hard gaze fell onto the doctor. "If you please, Mr. Hocking."

A funny expression crossed Doc's face as he held out his hand palm up to the statue.

Indy gasp as the Minotaur stepped lightly on to the waiting hand. Doc wrapped his fingers gently around it and pulled him to his chest.

"As you may have noticed these little creatures are quite protective. I found this Minotaur by my side since waking up in this room after the explosion. I'm not sure where he comes from but the company is most welcome."

Once the minotaur was secured, Jolie stepped forward and lowered her staff to the doctors exposed chest and said, "With any luck this should be our last session together Mr. Hocking. Try not to get yourself blown up again, okay?"

EDEN 14 – EXPERIMENTAL OCCUPATIONS

The entertainment room was busier than normal since the arrival of the radio equipment. Jon had set up Hank's old ham radio in a far corner of the room and equipped it with a 7.1 HD headset with boom microphone.

Joslyn had been sitting there for hours adjusting the settings back and forth while Indy and Jon sat on the couch playing video games. James walked into the room with a cheerful smile plastered on his face.

"Hello boys," he said and waved at Joslyn who nodded and went back to the dials. "Now that Doc Hocking has recovered from his injuries, he wants to show you his thanks for finding the latest stash of artifacts. He wants you three to meet him at the hydro plant if you want to see some of the artifacts in action."

"Really?" Jon was flabbergasted.

"Cool," Indy said. "What time does he want us there?"

"Anytime. He has cleared his schedule today in order to test out some of the newest toys." James looked around the entertainment room with a smile growing on his face. It was common knowledge around the castle that this was their hangout and the room was filled with everything a teenager could wish for.

The guys grinned at each other as they imagined the prospect of new adventures.

"You coming Joslyn?" Indy called, hoping to get her outside for at least a few minutes. She had been obsessed with the HAM unit since they got back from Hank's and hadn't been doing much else.

She looked over at them, smiled, and shook her head no.

"I'm heading down there now if you guys want a ride." James said giving Joslyn a wave as he led the boys from the room.

Indy had heard mention that the hydro plant was expanded and cleared out to make room for the artifacts. He hadn't seen the inside of the plant before because the doctor had requested that non-authorized people be kept out for safety reasons. Since the assault by the SEAL team the plants security had been increased, heavily increased.

As they entered the plant's main gate, Indy caught sight of people patrolling the rooftops and nearby grounds. Several of the guards carried assault rifles or other bundles Indy couldn't quite make out. Jon brushed Indy's shoulder and nodded at a tall antenna tower on the far side of the building. Long barrelled cameras mounted there turned to follow their progress across the lot.

"This place is like Fort Knox," Jon said under his breath.

Indy only nodded his head in agreement, as he thought about what his father had said. Maybe his dad wasn't as paranoid as he first thought.

James escorted them through a guard station and into the complex. They passed through one more guard station before walking into a large room that was hospital clean and painted bright white. Around the room, they could see hundreds of artifacts gleaming in the fluorescent lights. Each artifact had its own shelf or table and clipboard attached to it.

An older grey haired man stepped towards them as they gawked at the objects around the room.

"Hello. Welcome to Hydro," he said.

He pointed at the clipboards. "On those papers we write about the properties each artifact displays. Each clipboard is color-coded. Pay close attention to any details written in red. For your own safety, do not hold more than one artifact at a time. Henrik will be right with you, if you have any questions my name is Dr. Connor."

Dr. Connor stepped away quickly before they could even ask a single question. The man was smooth and precise but really needed to work on his people skills.

James laughed at the scientist as he walked away. "That guy just doesn't have a clue about what you two are about to get up to. Ok guys. I have to head back up to the house. But before I go, here's a little advice."

He pointed to the green clipboards. "Play with those ones first." James turned and walked from the room.

Before the door had even swung shut, the teenagers were moving. Within seconds, both of them had their hands on an artifact.

Jon had picked up a bumblebee shaped tube with dark glass on each end. Indy grabbed a leather cloth bundle that rippled with colors when he picked it up.

"Indy you gotta check this out," Jon said with awe in his voice. Jon fiddled with the tube as he looked through one end. "I can see about a hundred feet away with this thing. Through the wall and everything! Indy?"

Jon looked around. "Indy, where'd you go?" he asked with a tinge of worry. The air rippled in front of him as Indy pulled the hooded leather cloak off his head.

"No way! It's a chameleon cloak," Jon gasped.

The images displayed on the leather moved and swayed as Indy took it off.

"It must be some kind of active light refraction system. I could see right through you but as soon as you moved your image kinda blurred," Jon said as he fingered the thick leather cloak.

They spent the next hour playing with different artifacts as other people came and went from the room. Several people in lab coats brought bigger objects in and yet others took them away.

They were interrupted from their experiments when Doc Hocking came in from a door at the rear of the room.

"Ah. Thank you for coming boys," he said. "Please come with me."

They followed Doc down a long hallway and up a stairway. After a few minutes of walking, they finally entered a large office deep inside the plant. The office was crammed with odds and ends, there were skeletons, bubbling test tubes, and masonry jars filled with dark unmoving shapes.

The two young men looked around with curiosity until they noticed Sasser at work in a corner of the office. He had a small laptop plugged into a large TV screen.

"Are we ready Mr. Sasser?" Doc asked as they moved over to the TV.

"Yup. All keyed in. Hit play to start the sequence."

"Excellent, thank you for your expertise. You may go now." The doctor dismissed him with a wave.

Sasser looked a little confused but nodded his head and left the room. He spared a quick glance at Jon before he left.

"Before you ask me any questions, I have a little show for you to watch. You see, I may not have been completely honest in my reasons for inviting you here today. Although watching you two experiment with artifacts for the last hour or two was entertaining, I require some... thing else."

"But before we get to that I have some information I wish to share," Doc pointed at the TV and two nearby chairs.

"Sit," he said.

Worry and fear clouded Jon's face as they both sat in the offered chairs.

The Doc pressed play on the laptop and the screens lit up with images of Jon and his iPad.

"You both have been busy lately. Breaking into secure rooms and out late at night doing who knows what... like spying on the people of this castle. I wonder how people would react if they found out about these... hackers," Doc said the last word in a low whisper.

The screen had stopped on their favourite entertainment room. However, this time the angle of the camera was slightly different. The image showed Jon sitting on the couch, iPad in hand but it also showed a clear view of the TV screen just over his shoulder. The TV was flicking though different security cams while he watched.

"As you can see your hacking wasn't quite as complete as you might have believed."

"What do you want from me?" Jon begged, a dejected look spread across his face.

"Hahaha." The doctor's laugh was high and mocking. "From you, Jon, nothing."

The doctor's gaze slid to Indy as he paused the video.

"My dad won't..." Indy started to say.

A long finger cut the air for silence as the Hocking pressed play again.

This time it was a video montage of Indy.

It all started with the balcony jump and then cut to a thermal image view near some train tracks. The clip showed Indy's body flying over twenty feet in the air and skidding across the ground. Almost instantly, he was back on his feet.

The footage continued as Henrik Hocking spoke. "This next bit of film was harder to acquire, but thanks to some hard work by my team we got some really good stuff."

The footage was of a different man this time. He was outside a door holding two metal cans. The door was opened and the cans thrown inside. Two explosions quickly followed. As the camera went through the door, a machine gun barrel came into view.

The new angle showed the inside of the security operations room as people were falling to the floor with their eyes covered. All but one of the people inside dropped. Indy stood centered on the screen with a shocked look. Almost as quickly, his expression turned dark and angry.

The screen lit briefly with gunfire but in the next instant, the footage switched to slo-motion.

A bullet left the barrel of the gun like a hornet and smacked into Indy's chest. The image froze. Then it replayed again and again.

The doctor held up his hand to forestall any outburst. "Please let me explain what I want from you Mr. Locke."

"Your father has been pushing me and my team for weeks now. The man has been riding us hard for answers that we don't have. As far as we know we might not even be asking the right questions."

Doc sighed. "Anyway I need your help. I want you and your friends at the hydro plant every morning. We need you to help us... experiment."

"In return certain people will not learn of your transgressions," he looked pointedly at Jon.

"Or of your abilities." His gaze settled back on Indy. "Do we have a deal?" Doc Hocking asked politely.

Jon spoke up at once. "Sure. I guess it could be fun, hey Indy?"

Indy nodded slowly. Not liking the deal but seeing little choice. He had intended on telling his parents the moment he realized the power he held. At first, he didn't want to worry them but after he had seen the proud look on his father's face when he saved Joslyn. Well, he didn't want to lose that. Indy came to a decision, he would tell his father the next time he had a chance. In the meantime, he wanted to get a better look around the hydro plant, and this was the perfect excuse.

EDEN 15 - FLYBOYS

For Jon and Indy the next few days were a grand adventure. Indy was poked and prodded in a hundred different ways. Scientists blasted him with everything and anything they could imagine. They tried pressure, high torque collision, heavy weights, electricity, and even a laser.

Nothing penetrated his skin. But, one thing they did learn early on was that his clothing wasn't able to withstand the same tortures. His best pair of jeans was now just a pile of ash after he was introduced to a flamethrower.

For Jon it was a totally different ball game. Doc Hocking found his thinking creative and outside the box. He had been given free rein among the artifacts to explore in hopes of finding something the others might have missed.

Today Jon was working his way around the room, finding new toys to play with and even trying to combine multiple artifact effects. Joslyn had elected to stay up at the castle yet again. She was still trying to get a signal through the communications blackout to her loved ones.

Indy watched Jon from a chair in the center of the experiment room. A lab tech was buzzing around him trying to check Indy's reflexes.

Jon was on his last artifact in the room with a green clipboard. This artifact was a small metal hoop that had two small horns at the top.

Jon picked it up and studied it a moment. He waved it around a few times then tapped it with his other hand. Nothing happened.

"Hmmm," Jon hummed to himself and then gave in a little quicker than usual this time and peeked at the instructions on the clipboard.

"Oh I would have got it," he muttered.

Jon squeezed the horns together and a rope of white silk flew from the single horn straight at Indy as he lifted a water bottle. The bottle was half way to his lips when the silk rope struck with a wet plop.

Indy saw Jon's evil grin a second too late as his friend yanked the bottle from his hands. Water splashed over him soaking his hair and shorts.

"Jon! You little jerk," Indy shouted.

Indy stood and the technician assisting him took cover. Jon laughed as the bottle came sailing back to him. His laugh was cut short as the water bottle collided with the artifact ring and splashed him too. His shirt was drenched. The tech came over quickly with a towel as the boys laughed at each other's mishap. He helped to mop up the water and disengaged the bottle from the ring.

"Give me that shirt and I'll go dry it for you," he told Jon.

Another tech had come back in through a side door with two bundles of clothes. "Ah, good timing, Doc wants you two to get these suits on and head outside," he said and handed both bundles over. Inside the bundles were two flight suits and two large black helmets.

131

Doctor Hocking came in moments after with Zeus following in his wake. "Excellent. I see you two are almost ready. Finish suiting up and meet us outside when you are ready. We have a little surprise for you today."

Excitement bursting through every pore, they stripped from their wet cloths and zipped into a one-piece leather jumpsuit. Each had a pair of thin gloves and soft leather boots.

"You totally look badass dude," Jon told Indy.

"You too Jon," Indy grinned.

They swaggered from the room like two fighter pilots.

Outside the techs were gathered around two sleek black sleds. The sleds were all smooth twisting curves and hard lines. Light blue gel filled the sleds interior with a soft glow.

Doc Hocking stood over the two sleds and gestured down at them. "We call these two beauties AGPs or Anti-gravity personnel sleds. The techs will help you into them and please listen carefully to their instructions. They are yet untested but we wanted to thank you two for all the help you have given us these last few days."

One of the techs instructed Indy to lie down on his belly. As he lowered himself in the gel softened and then wrapped around his body.

The tech continued to lecture him in the sleds dynamics. "The gel acts like a shock absorber and seat belt. Now put your hands and feet into these four pockets. Good. Your flight controls are at the four corners. Feet up or down and bank left or right. Your hands turn left or right and control the speed. Think of it like this. Stretching out makes, you go up fast. Curling in slows you down and lowers you."

"Don't worry too much, the sleds have some kind of safety system built in. You won't hit anything even if you try. It will also bring you back down safely if you manage to pass out from the g-forces."

"Got it?" the tech asked.

Indy nodded yes.

"The AGPs turn on by wiggling your fingers and toes. Good. Now remember stay inside the aurora and don't go too high. You don't have any oxygen on board. The tech stepped away and gave him the thumbs up."

"Too high?" Indy's voice broke.

He looked over at Jon who has just started his own sled.

Brumpt brumpt brump brump. The sleds power reverberated through his core.

Jon's sled rose smoothly from the ground and then rocketed up into the sky.

A shadow fell over Indy and he looked up. Zeus stood over him and looked down with an evil stare. The man had a way of popping up at the worst times.

"Go ahead Indy," he said. "Not still scared of heights are ya?"

Indy hesitated a moment longer, despising that man a little more before he activated the sled and shot forward and up slightly.

The techs scattered but Zeus held his ground as the sled raced by.

Doc turned to the techs as the sleds grew to specks in the distance. "You two go inside and take care of that mess, that mixture was watered down but still very corrosive. Burn the clothes, just in case," Doc snarled. He turned to Zeus. "Call up to the house and have some fresh cloths delivered before the boys get back."

MARTY LONGSON

EDEN 16 – THE GROWING OF TREES

Two sleek black sleds rocketed over the coastal ridge, racing hard against the wind. The AGPs were fast. Indy might be scared of heights but not speed. He lived for that. He watched Jon bank, dive, roll, and spin high above. However, Indy's flight path kept him just under ten feet off the ground.

He could hear Jon's laughter filling his ears as his friend buzzed around above. "Dude, I can hear you laughing. These helmets have hands free microphones," Indy said into his own microphone.

The laughter abruptly stopped. "Really? Do you think anyone else can hear us?" Jon asked quietly.

"Probably. If not I'm sure they are recording it," Indy said as he watched the ground fly by below him.

"Anyone out there copy this?" Jon's voice asked over airwaves.

A stern voice spoke in their ears in response. "Roger that little pigs 1 and 2. This is big bad wolf on channel 1. We got eyes and ears on you two."

"Copy that wolf," Jon said realizing his fun was being monitored.

"Little pigs please feel free to vocalize any data. This is a test after all." The voice called big bad wolf ordered.

135

"Ok we get the message. Little pig 1, out," Jon said as he assumed the role of little pig 1.

"Ok Indy, Let's see what these babies can do," Jon shouted.

Indy agreed and stretched out fully reaching out with fingers and toes. Instantly the sled raced forward rising slightly. He tried some easy turns and found the control exact and precise.

A boulder came out of nowhere. Well at least at that speed it appeared to. The sled instantly recalibrated and raised Indy's sled higher by a few inches as he passed over the boulder.

"Incredible," he thought.

The next few minutes flew by with Indy and Jon buzzing around the grounds, taking runs at obstacles just to see how the sleds reacted. Indy was still low on the ground weaving and turning in long sweeping circles. He raced toward a stand of tall trees. They came at him fast and the sled bobbed, weaved, and twisted through them without touching a single branch.

"I wish my bike could do that," Indy said, slowing down to look back at the stand of trees. He felt a hollow knock on his helmet.

"Tag. Your it," Jon's laughter filled his ears again.

Indy turned to look up. He saw Jon hovering just above him... Upside down!

The other sled lifted and turned away, racing back towards the hydro plant and castle.

"Come down here if you want a real game little pig 1." Indy cursed over the microphone.

More laughter filled his ears as the other sled came around aiming right at him. The two sleds raced towards each other before veering away automatically.

"You are crazy," Indy berated Jon.

"Ya and you are still it," Jon said with more mocking laughter.

They played cat and mouse for a few minutes before Indy called for a stop. They had just passed over a wide stream when he had noticed his mother below. Jolie Locke was sitting on the edge of the river with her feet and staff in the water. Indy stopped above her and watched as she stirred the water with the white staff. The whole time he hovered there his mom never once looked up.

"Indy what's up with your mom?" Jon asked. "She okay?"

Indy agreed that something wasn't right. "I'm putting down over there," he said. "Little pig 2 over and out."

Indy set down the sled and took his helmet off. Once the helmet was off, he was able to hear his mom singing softly. The air seemed to vibrate around him as he listened to her soothing song.

"Mom," he said as he touched her shoulder. "Are you ok?"

His mom stopped singing and looked up at him.

"Junior? What is it? Can you hear the trees? They are crying out in pain. At first, I could only hear them in my sleep. It was like a bad dream that would never end. Now I hear them when I am awake. Even the water is speaking to me now. Is that why you have come?" her voice almost sung to him it was so sweet and mournful at the same time.

"No mom, I don't hear it. I don't hear anything."

"I'm sorry Daniel. It's so beautiful and yet at the same time so full of pain. I think they are trying to tell me something."

He nodded at her and she started to sing again. As he watched her start to stir the water again his mom seemed to forget he was even there. He stood there for a while just listening to her sweet song and watching her swirl the waters with the white staff.

A twig snapping behind him broke the spell and he turned to see James standing in the shadow of a tree. "Your mom's been acting like this for a few days now," he said. "Your dad says she's been staying outside for days on end. She's even sleeping out here now. Your father spends as much time as he can watching over her, but he does have matters he must attend to. Maybe she's just feeling cooped up especially now that there isn't any one left that needs healing."

"Ya, I hope so," Indy said. "I just hate to see her like that. It makes me worry about her. You know what I mean. Can I do anything for her?"

"Sure. Sleep outside with her tonight. My back could use a nice firm mattress tonight. Maybe you just being around will help."

"You think its depression?" Indy asked.

"Maybe. Maybe not, it's hard to say. This whole mess has us down the rabbit hole." James said.

"Down the rabbit hole?" Indy asked.

"Ha-ha. It's just a figure of speech Indy."

Indy nodded and said. "Ok I will see you tonight, thank you James. You're a good man."

James dipped his head once and leaned back against the tree to resume his watch.

Indy walked slowly back to the AGP, looking back several times at his mom. He slid back onto the gel padding and activated the sled. As he rose up to where Jon was waiting for him, he considered his mom's words.

"Ready dude?" Jon asked quietly, bringing Indy out of his daze.

Indy nodded his dark helmet.

"Look it's getting late, we should head back. Follow me." Jon took off without looking to see if he followed.

Indy took off heading back to the hydro plant but looked back at his mom one more time before he left. She was still sitting beside the water, staff in hand and a song moving her lips.

EDEN 17 – INDY'S LULLABY

Indy and his mom slept under the stars that night. It was a beautiful night and they talked for hours. She recalled his past exploits and brazen late night fridge raids. Indy reminded her of all the great times he had with her growing up. It was the most they had talked in years. He made a silent vow to spend more time with her in the future. There was no way he would let them grow any further apart. He would make time for his parents, just as his father asked.

"I love you Indy. I want you to remember that, no matter what," she told him quietly.

"Of course mom. I love you too."

Jolie looked up into the sky and watched as the multi coloured aurora danced across the heavens. "I don't know who to thank for this miracle we have been given. But I feel we are truly blessed," she looked happily at him. This staff, I think has given me a second chance at life. But there is more to it than that. I think it's meant for something else, something much more then healing a broken soul like me."

"What do you mean mom?"

"Let me show you," she said.

Jolie searched around on the ground for a moment looking and finding a discarded peach pit.

"Ahh here we go, watch closely." she said as she stood over the little peach pit and put both hands on the staff. The staff instantly glowed blue. She lowered the tip of the staff down until it pushed the seed into the soft earth.

The staffs light started to pulse. Slow at first then faster. It sounded like a heart beating. Tiny sprouts popped from the spot the pit had sunken into. They grew faster than Indy's eyes could follow. It was pure magic, in an instant it was a sapling, then a small tree and finally a full-grown tree stood before them. The white staff jutted out from the base of the new tree.

When Jolie tugged on the staff, it came out easily but left a small hole in the trunk from where the wood had grown around it.

"It wasn't meant just to heal us Daniel. This is meant to heal the world."

Indy's face must have betrayed something he didn't realize.

His mom looked sadly at him.

"No you don't see it either. Your father couldn't understand what this means," he r voice seemed to falter as the sadness touched her eyes. "Everything we have found in this valley is here for a reason," she said. "This staff, the storage room, and even the aurora that keeps us here."

"Mom I'm not sure what these things are. Even if we don't understand what makes them work, I doubt there is anything here that's going to change the world. Doc said that most of these artifacts were nothing but kid's toys. That they really weren't able to doing much with them."

Jolie's look had turned sour at the mention of Doc's name. "Don't trust that man Daniel. He came highly recommended from other people we trust. But I can see something in his eyes. A lust for power or just pure greed, I don't know."

"Did you tell dad how you feel about him?" Indy asked.

"Oh your father knows. But he is choosing to overlook some things in order to get his answers. So far Henrik Hocking has been the only person to consistently bring results."

"But you don't like him," Indy stated bluntly.

"No Daniel. I do not," she agreed.

They sat quietly for a time, Indy mulling over his mother's words.

He finally asked her what had been nagging at the back of his mind. "When you said the staff is meant to heal the world... what do you mean?"

She regarded her son closely for a long moment before a smile formed on her face. "Well, when I stumbled onto the staff being able to help grow seeds, I started to wonder if it could help heal plants too."

"Can it?" Indy asked.

"Just look around us. This area was devastated just days ago by that cruise missile. I used the staff to revive plants destroyed or burned by the explosion. All the metal and contaminants have been cleansed from the soil and absorbed into the plants themselves."

"I can assure you that this staff is important for all of us," she told him, her voice firm and steady. "In fact it is this staff that will save our planet from our own destructive ways."

"Ha-ha," Indy laughed aloud. "When did you become a tree hugger mom?"

"Daniel Locke junior I expect you to listen closely." His mother scolded. "This staff has changed the way I see the world around us. When I hold it, I can see decay and poisons on the ground and in the air. I can look at a person or plant and see the cancers of this world that are killing each of us slowly. Like a river wearing away the rock below it. Our people will die just as the plants and trees are dying around the world right now."

"So what can we do about it?" Indy said in a hushed voice. It had been a very long time since his mother had talked to him like that or since she had held such firm resolve in her voice. It made him sit up a little straighter and listen a little closer to her words.

"I think whoever made this staff and the aurora that surrounds this valley had a plan. Maybe it was a kind of emergency response or a reset button to avoid our ultimate destruction. The room we found this staff in… it had other places listed, maybe other situations would activate them. I believe that whoever made this… aurora was brilliant even beyond our scope of imagination."

"Why?" he asked.

"I think all of this was a plan. From the sinkhole that led your father to that room, to Mr. Hocking's so called childish toys that taught us how to learn and use this unknown power. Each step has led us down this path, slowly and carefully."

"You mean like FEMAS emergency disaster relief plan?" Indy asked.

His mom burst out laughing. "Yes, I suppose you could compare it to FEMA. But I am still not exactly sure who will be saved. It may be the world that we save or the staff might only save who ever lives with us, within the auroras protection. Like a Noah's ark if you will."

"How are we going to save anyone? I mean do you have any idea what to do?"

"That is a discussion for another night," Jolie said as she started to yawn. "Go to sleep son and dream sweet dreams. I have a few things to think over before I go to sleep."

She walked over to him and bent to kiss his forehead. She then turned to walk to the edge of the stream and as she went, he heard her start humming a soft lullaby.

He closed his eyes as she sat down and he listened to the wordless hum of her voice as he drifted off to sleep.

EDEN 18 – LAST LETTERS

When Indy woke in the morning, he was alone. He scanned the area for his mom but she was nowhere to be found. There was an envelope next to his sleeping bag. A ripe peach sat on top of the envelope, holding it in place. He tore open the envelope and then read the letter inside.

Dearest Son,

If you are reading this then I did not return before you woke, as I had hoped. I left in the night as you slept and walked to the coast. I know the staff I carry is a heavy burden but one I carry as easily as a feather. I have understood for days now that this staff is not just a wooden stick. It is a seed to something great and powerful. As you lay sleeping, I plan to plant it much the same way I did the peach pit last night. This time however, I worry that the seed may grow up around me, enclosing me within it. The seed and I have a deeply rooted bond, we have become entwined, and the power I feel in my bones is awesome. I fear that neither of us can function now without the other. I go now in hope to ensure my family has a bright future. I really don't know what tomorrow will bring, but if my sacrifice is needed to achieve my goals, I do it willingly for you and your father.

With your life, I have loved. With your love, I have life.

Please forgive me for not saying goodbye. I could not stand the pain lest it break my will and resolve. I could not chance anyone talking me out of this. So I will say it here instead, goodbye son and remember I love you.

P.S. take care of your father. He will need you now more than ever.

Indy was crying as he read the letter and up and running as he finished reading. The paper fluttering to the ground as he headed up the trail towards the coast. Wisps of white morning fog swirled around his ankles as he ran through the trees.

He saw it before he was through the tree line. A gigantic towering white tree with dark brown leaves. The brown leaves reminded him of his mother's silky long hair and the pale white bark, like her fair skin. Tears streamed down his face as he ran harder towards the tree.

As he ran closer, he spotted his father and James near the base of the tree. His father kneeled before the tree with his head bowed. James stood just behind him with a piece of paper clutched tightly to his chest.

He could hear his dad murmuring as he grew closer. "My Jolie. My Jolie. Why. Why, did you leave me?"

Indy looked up at the tall tree. It was easily as big as the largest of the redwoods. It was as wide as a bus and its roots ran thick and deep into the rocky ridge overlooking the coast. Deep clouds of fog had rolled in during the night, covering the ocean in fluffy white clouds. It gave the morning an eerie surreal feeling.

He reached for his dad.

James stopped him with a gentle hand on his shoulder.

Indy shook off the hand and called to his dad, "Dad. Is she... in there?"

The murmurs stopped as his dad spoke with a raspy voice. "Touch the tree and hear for yourself."

Indy moved to the tree and reached out his hand. He felt... nothing, his protective skin failed to communicate even the texture of the white wood. But he kept his hand there and pressed his ear close to listen.

He could hear a gentle humming that reminded him of his mom's lullaby.

"Mom!" he cried. Indy sank to the ground in a posture that mimicked his fathers.

"James," Daniel Locke said over his shoulder. "Go back to the castle and prepare a statement. My son and I need to be alone for a while."

"Yes sir." James said stiffly and stomped off.

"Indy, come over here." His dad stood and motioned him to follow.

It was the first time his dad had ever called him Indy and the significance was great in Indy's mind.

They walked around the tree until they came to the side that faced the ocean. A few of the large roots here were bent to form a sort of sitting area.

"Sit," he said and patted one of the large roots beside him.

Indy sat.

They sat there and stared out to sea as the breeze blew through the leaves of Jolie's hair and the rumble of the surf drowned out the lullaby from their ears but not their souls.

EDEN 19 – UNINVITED GUESTS

Even though Jolie Locke wasn't actually dead, everyone was in grief. A dark cloud seemed to settle around everyone in the castle. Indy watched his father falter and lose direction.

It was Dr. Henrik Hocking that filled the leadership role left by the grieving Daniel Locke Senior. When Daniel disappeared from public life, Doc stepped up to take his place. Many people began to look to Henrik to find solutions to daily problems. Others simply disappeared to their rooms, choosing instead to deal with their own issues personally.

The doctor gained more supporters when he began to release some of the artifacts he had been studying. Several of the green artifacts had been released from the experiments room and he had his son Warren showing them off whenever he could. People started lining up early in the morning for a chance to borrow one of the artifacts for a day.

Warren Hocking became an overnight celebrity in the castle. Every night he would host a small demonstration on the sports fields. Each night began to be more extravagant then the last. Warren would finish the show with a long blowgun artifact that shot fireworks into the sky. Crowds began to gather hours before he began, in order to get the best seats. The artifacts he used stunned and wowed everyone in the crowd. People cheered him in the hallways of the castle and the kid's ego grew to match.

Indy walked into the kitchens after dinner one evening as Warren and his friends were entertaining the cooking staff with an artifact light show. It seemed like Warren's little posse had grown overnight and included most of his teammates from the king's court game he had interrupted previously. In fact, now that he thought about it, this was the first time Indy had come across Warren since that day on the fields. As he watched the light show from the doorway, he noticed Amber Crombly and Thomas Walker casting dark glances his way.

Earlier that day Jon had just been telling Indy about this little posse of Warren's. Out of the whole group of kids, Jon had warned Indy to watch out for these two above all else. They had been known to cause trouble for all the kids around the castle at one time or another. Jon had called them practical jokers, but each of them had a big mean streak a mile wide and an ego to match.

Amber stood glaring at him through dark horn rimmed glasses that were framed by her pin straight long black hair. She was the picture perfect image of a Goth girl, thin and wiry. She wore black clothes, black nail polish with black lipstick and eyeliner.

Thomas Walker was a different creature, in fact he resembled a gorilla. Short and squat with thick arms and a barrel chest. He was dressed like most other kids in jeans and a shirt but neither fit him right. His shirt was too tight and his jeans were big and baggie to the point of falling off his butt.

When Thomas spotted Indy in the door, he strolled over to whisper something in Warren's ear. Warren looked in

Indy's direction and nodded once with a slight smile. Warren then fished a small silver object out of his pocket and handed it to Thomas. With a grin, Thomas walked back to Amber and then started his way.

Indy knew from the short stocky kid's glare there was going to be trouble, so he stepped out of the kitchen and into the hallway, out of view of the cooks.

A few moments later Thomas stepped into the hall with Amber trailing in his wake. "Warren wants me to deliver a little message to you," Thomas said as he balled his fists.

Indy was just about to step forward to meet the challenge when Amber stepped in front of Thomas. "Whoa, relax boys," she said in a sweet soft voice. "Warren just wanted me to deliver this to you. A little peace offering I think." Amber held out a closed hand.

Indy reached for the gift without looking and somewhere inside it occurred to him that Amber's expression didn't match up with her sweet voice. She was hiding something from him. He found out what it was when she slapped a silver spider into his open palm.

The silver spider broke apart in his hand and hundreds of tiny black spiders started to course over his skin. In their wake, they trailed lines of a sticky white web.

Indy tried to shake the spiders loose but the was too many of them and they moved too fast. He tried brushing them off with his other hand but they ended up sticking to that hand as well.

Thomas and Amber stepped back and watched Indy as he was wrapped in the thin webbing. In moments, his body was covered head to toe and he fell backwards onto the floor, unable to move his arms or legs. Indy could hear mocking laughter as the pair of kids circled him, taunting him as he lay helpless and stuck to the floor.

"Warren wanted us to tell you he says, hi," Thomas said.

"If you want to stick around he will be back sometime tomorrow," Amber added with a hoarse laugh.

Indy heard her bend down to pick something up off the floor and then only their footsteps as they walked away.

Indy laid there for what felt like hours until he heard someone else approaching. He couldn't even call out for help except in a low quiet mumble. Luckily, he was easy to spot since he was right in the middle of the hall and he heard Allen's voice call out to him.

"Who's in there?" Allen asked.

"mmmfff mmmme, mmmmddeeee" was Indy's only response.

"Indy?" Allen said. "Hang on, I know what to do. I'll go get something to get you out." Allen's footsteps raced away and were back in seconds.

When Allen finally got back, he was out of breath. "Warren pulled that trick on me last night when I was coming back from the soccer fields. I guess I was just lucky, but I figured out how to get out…" Allen said as he dumped a large bucket of water over Indy's webbed body. "…salt water! Well in my case it was sweat, but it's basically the same thing."

When the water hit the web, the webbing instantly dissolved from Indy, like cotton candy in a rainstorm. Indy got slowly to his feet and pulled long thick bunches of clumped webbing from his soaked clothes.

"Thanks Allen, I owe you one," Indy said and patted Allen on the back, trying not to get any of the webbing on his friend.

"You are welcome Indy," Allen said with a wide smile.

"Don't worry about Warren, he will get what's coming to him soon enough," Allen said as he helped Indy brush off the last of the webs. "Karma has a way of coming back to haunt you."

The entertainment room was quiet as Indy passed through heading to the open balcony doors. The incident with Warren's friends really didn't bother him much. It was just another hurdle in an already bad day. After a quick shower and a change of clothes, Indy just needed some peace and quiet. So when Jon and Joslyn had gone out to climb the white tree, eager to see how high they could get, Indy declined their invitation. He told them he had a headache and needed to relax, which wasn't far from the truth.

Indy stared out across the grounds as he stood on the balcony breathing deep and trying to relax. In the distance, the great white tree had continued to grow and flourish. The massive tree rippled in the sunlight as a light wind came off the ocean. At this distance, he could see several grounds keepers and scientists working around the base of the white tree. Indy looked up at the crown of the tree and marvelled at its odd dark brown leaves. Indy had watched while others had climbed up the twisting trunk with its deeply grooved bark but hadn't gotten the nerve up to try it for himself.

Joslyn and Jon were out there now on the lowest branches trying to collect some of the large brown leaves. Even the leaves of the tree were massive. Each leaf had to be at least four feet long from stem to tip. As far as he could tell, the strong leaves had resisted all efforts to pull them free.

A flash high in the sky caused him to look up. Something had hit the aurora high in the air above them and the warning sirens started to wail. Indy stared up trying to see what had happened. He could see a cloud of fire and several dark shapes dropping from the sky. They fell for about thirty seconds before little black parachutes popped out above them. He watched as the chutes swirled high above the castle and drift out over the forest below.

The intercom cracked high in the corner of the room. "Red alert. Red alert. We have possible hostile's incoming. Castle defenders to your stations. This is not a drill." Indy ran from the room and headed up to the security station.

Sasser was there hands dancing over his keyboard and monitoring the incoming chutes. He was speaking into a microphone as Indy ran in. "Roger Zeus, confirm six chutes. Looks like the debris didn't make it into the aurora, it's raining into the pacific as I watch."

Zeus voice crackled over the speakers. "Keep an eye on those chutes. My team is standing by."

Another voice chimed in. "Doc Hocking here. Zeus, I want those people taken into custody as soon as they land. Bring them to the Hydro station once you have them. We have a few rooms down here that can serve as holding cells if need be."

"Yes Sir, Doc," Zeus replied. "We are standing by but it looks like several of the chutes will be coming down closer to the quarry. We are tracking six chutes so far."

"I don't care how you do it," Doc said with an edge of anger in his voice. "Just make sure you contain them before they can do any damage. Doc out."

"Ok Zeus, the chutes are almost down," Sasser said. "We have two sets of three. Three near the quarry came down in the trees. The other set of three set down near the water caves. Looks like they are gonna make a try for the Hydro station. Wait, what's that... Zeus they have weapons. I am seeing several AK-47s."

"You get a visual ID on their faces yet," Zeus's voice was calm and demanding.

Sasser banged the keyboard around. "Hang on, software's coming up now. Facial recognition running...local database is loading..."

"And?" Zeus demanded.

"Ok its up," Sasser breathed in deep as he watched his computer work. "Looks like they are Chinese Military, maybe another Special Forces team...Doc, come in."

"Doc here."

"Doc, did you copy that last bit," Sasser asked.

"Of course I did. The Hydro's defenses are online. Zeus keep your team back and observe."

"Yes sir," Zeus replied.

Sasser switched the screens and the hydro station appeared. Three dark shapes were moving in from the left side of the screen when the defenses kicked it. A few of Doc's team were suited up in the artifact armour and were holding several long rods in their hands. AK-47s make a very distinctive sound when fired and Indy could hear the chatter in the distance. The dark figures on the screen had taken cover and were using the AK-47s with practised ease. The scientists moved forward with no visible reaction to the shots. They were within several hundred feet of the intruders when the rods in their hands started to glow.

Long strings of purple rope started to flow out from the rods. The rope dipped and swayed like racing eels as it danced towards the intruders. The purple rope struck with an electric clap as the ropes entangled the intruders and dropped them like sacks. The armoured scientists on the screen were moving in when Sasser turned to look at Indy. Shock and awe were evident on his face.

"Team one report," Zeus called out.

"Team one here." Was the response. "The quarry is clear. Tangos DOA. Looks like they didn't make it from the plane, the chutes must have been on automated release."

"Roger Team one. Bring the bodies and their equipment to Doc at the hydro plant."

"Team Two Report."

"Team two here." Someone said. "The defenses are intact and Tangos are in custody. No injuries to report."

"Roger Team two. Good work. Have an escort sent in and put them in the cells we can have someone…"

"Thank you Zeus but my team will take it from here. We have it all under control."

"Yes sir. Zeus over and out," Zeus said his voice harsh and indignant.

Indy watched as Sasser shook his head and clicked off the microphone and several screens.

"What's up Sasser?" Indy said. "You look a bit pissed."

The man looked at Indy. A dark sour look crossed his face.

"Without your dad around that Doc guy has been stepping up his game. He is putting everyone in his pocket one way or another. The man is bossing us around like he is the one paying our salaries. I don't mean to be rude but… You need to have a word with your dad. I've tried a couple times but James keeps turning me away from your dad's rooms."

"He is grieving, give him time," Indy said. "My mom had just come back to us and he is having a hard time accepting she is gone. I think he blames me in a way. Like I could have stopped her or something."

"You couldn't have done anything Indy. Your mom made her decision. She knew what she was doing and she knew how many people it could save in the end. I admire her for that."

"You mean hopefully save," Indy said in a low voice. "She's a tree now. What good can one tree do? I know it's a big tree but still. Its only one tree."

Sasser looked him for a moment with a deep sadness in his eyes. "I don't have any answers for you. All I know is that this place is something special. Before your Mom left us, everyone in here felt it. We were excited and there was energy in everyone's step. I know, I sit here and watch people day in and day out on these screens. I have seen things that I can only explain with one word. MAGIC."

The word hung in the air between them for a minute as they both considered the possibilities.

Sasser was the first to speak again. "If it's not magic, I'm not sure what it is but I know that there isn't a better explanation right now than that. Before the aurora materialized, I watched people wander around depressed and lonely. I have seen people half dead and lost in their own world. This place has slowly changed that. People are helping each other, no matter the cost or the time involved. For a long time there, we were making real progress making this a real community."

"And now?" Indy asked.

"Well, now things are changing again. Zeus is running around here like we are his own little private army and Doc has that plant bottled up to hide his little secrets."

"Doc?" Indy said quietly.

"Yeah, he thinks your dad isn't a good leader. He wants us ready for a coming storm, whatever that means. I have been watching him for the last couple of days. Haven't you noticed him and his little band of followers?"

"Ya," Indy grunted. "I saw a bunch of them down in the kitchens earlier. Warren was showing off some artifacts to the cooks."

Sasser looked around the room before he said anything. "I don't really want to say too much but that isn't all he has been up to."

"What is he up to?" Indy demanded.

"I really can't say what his goal is. But I have seen a few messages being relayed from the barricade teams straight to his hand."

Indy was stunned. "He is getting messages in and out? What about the rest of us? What have they been saying about us? Did you get a newspaper or anything?"

"Whoa Indy... slow down. As far as I know its official military correspondence. From one of the higher ups, I think his name was Colonel Tapper. Doc hasn't been keeping me in the loop lately. He has been playing his cards pretty close to his chest.

Just keep an eye on him and tell your dad what you see. It would be better if you see things with your own eyes and come to your own conclusions. Try to get Daniel out of his

depression.   Maybe get him to mingle with ever one else
again."

"Ok, thanks Sasser. I'll see what I can do."

Indy walked back into the entertainment room at the same
time as Jon and Joslyn.

"Did you hear about the intruders?" Indy asked them.

"No," Jon said. But we saw Zeus running for the jeeps
when we got back. The sirens started going off so we went to
the barracks with Allen and some of his friends."

"So what happened?" Joslyn asked.

Indy told them about the Chinese soldiers and the firefight
at the hydro station.

Jon was stunned. "The scientists? In armour?"

"Yeah and they had these really cool energy whips too.
They had those guys wrapped up in minutes. It was kinda
scary. Indy shook his head. We never saw any whips or any
other kind of weapons in the experiment room. I have a
feeling we didn't get to see half of the stuff the Doc has
stashed away."

The radio in the corner started to crackle and pop. Joslyn
ran over to it and tweaked some settings.

- Radio BBC is reporting Live from the news center in
London…

- The US aircraft carrier "JOHN F KENNEDY" has
come under attack from an unknown source. Many analysts
are pointing their fingers at the Chinese Military after a stealth
attack plane crashed in the Pacific Ocean earlier today.

- Reports have come in stating that the attack resulted in
heavy U.S. casualties and the loss of several jets and navy

boats. In recent days, the U.S. had come under heavy criticism for their handling of what is now being referred to as the Eden Valley in Northern California. Russia and China both have been arguing for an international task force to oversee the investigation of the aurora that appeared in the region several weeks ago. The U.S. has maintained the media blackout regarding the flow of all information relating to the aurora and the people trapped within. The international community demands have been pressuring the U.S. to allow other countries the opportunity to study the aurora phenomenon and the mysteries held within.

- The President is expected to release a statement later today announcing possible sanctions or actions against all parties responsible for the attack.

- NATO has upgraded its DEFCON level to the highest it has been since the Cuban missile crisis in 1962.

The radio went silent for a minute before Joslyn tried adjusting the dials. "We must have gotten a bounce. The signals are still being jammed. I can't get anything else."

"Keep trying Joslyn. Jon, I need a favour. Can you set something up with that little pad of yours?"

"Sure, whatcha need?" Jon's face broadened with a large smile.

"I need you to keep an eye on Doc. Make sure you record it all and put it on a flash drive for me. I want to see where he is and what he is doing ever second of the day."

"Why, what's going on Indy?" Joslyn asked.

Indy debated about telling her his fears. "Let's just say that I don't trust Doc. I think he knows a lot more about what's going on here then he's letting on. He is purposely keeping my dad in the dark and making him look like a fool. That man is up to something, we just have to figure out what it is."

EDEN 20 – MINI HOUDINI

They spent the next couple of days watching Doc Hocking on Jon's hacked video feed. Most of the original security cameras were destroyed or inactive in the experiments building, other than those covering the main room. Doc spent the bulk of his day outside of camera view. As far as Indy could tell, the man was an awkward social butterfly. At times, he seemed to wander around in any given direction and stop almost every person he ran across. More often than not Doc Hocking would stay late into the evening hours locked away inside his lab where the kids could not see him. They continued to watch the monitors in shifts, looking for anything out of the ordinary.

"This is impossible," Jon complained. "There has to be a better way than this. Even if the man was building a nuclear bomb in that lab we would never know."

Indy and Joslyn both agreed they needed to be able to see into the labs. The problem was that the whole area had some major security. They sat watching the experiments room feed as Warren came into view of the cameras. In his hands, he held two artifacts. One was a blue ball that glowed with static electricity and the other was a long leather cloak that swirled with color.

Jon sat forward suddenly and stared intently at the TV. I've got it! He yelled at the screen. "Take the ball, take the ball," Jon chanted under his breath. "Take the ball you stupid piece of Bantha fodder."

Indy and Joslyn watched with mixed expressions of humour and curiosity as Jon became more and more animated. Excitement filled Jon as Warren chose the electrified ball.

"Yes, that's it noobie. Take your little ball and go," Jon smiled at them. "I've got a plan."

The experiments room was devoid of people as the guard let Indy, Jon, and Joslyn in.

"The Doc will be pretty happy you two decided to come back," he was saying. "The man's been pretty depressed since the lab blew up. A lot of people have stopped coming by, I guess they are afraid of something else blowing up the place."

The guard nodded at Jon and turned to leave. Indy swore he saw the guard wink slightly as he was leaving.

They waited until the doors were closed before they started showing Joslyn around the room. Indy showed off a few of his favourite artifacts first. Jon meanwhile was browsing artifacts along a different wall. He was pulling artifacts out as he moved along the tables only to put them down again when he saw something else that caught his eye. Only a few minutes into the artifact demonstrations Joslyn grew bored.

She crossed her arms and pouted. "Are we done yet?"

"Just a few more things, I promise," Indy said. "Jon wanted to show you some of his favourites too."

Jon called them over and began showing Joslyn the artifacts he had collected. All his favourites seemed to be big and loud. Still disinterested Joslyn merely bent over the tables as Jon pointed at the artifacts he had arranged for her. Joslyn kept her arms crossed and pouted the whole time.

"Ok, are we done now?" she said more than asked.

The three of them agreed that they were done and headed for the exit. They almost walked right into Warren as he came into the room.

"What are you three doing here? My dad said the experiment room is off limits until we figure out what caused the explosion."

"Relax Warren," Jon said. "Joslyn didn't get a chance to look at this stuff yet. We just gave her a little tour."

Warren looked at Joslyn who still had her arms cross but now wore a distasteful expression. "It would have been nice if someone would have volunteered to show me around here sooner," she gave Warren a little sweeter lingering look and then looked away, with her crystalized hair flipping over to cover her milky blue eye.

Indy started to push past Warren when he was grabbed by the arm. Warren leaned in close and whispered into Indy's ear. "I haven't forgotten about your big mouth, you little rich snob. If you ever pull a stunt like that again, I'll take it out on one of these two."

Indy looked hard at the bully and suddenly realized that Warren knew all about his ability. Doc must have mentioned something about it to his son. This wasn't the time for this and Indy had to resist making a scene. "I understand," he said under his breath and pulled free from Warren's grasp. Warren pushed past and left the three standing there in the doorway watching him leave.

"That was close," Joslyn whispered.

"Shhh," Indy urged her.

The walked through the door and waved to the guard on the other side before making their way back to the Razor ATV.

They all hopped into the ATV but when Joslyn got in there was a loud clanking noise.

Jon started giggling uncontrollably and Indy smiled wide. "Nice work Joslyn."

In the back seat, Joslyn opened her impromptu invisibility bag. Inside the folded leather cloak, she had managed to hide a handful of artifacts. She had grabbed the telescope, the angel sword, a horned metal ring, and a couple crystal globes.

"Once I got the telescope and sword in the bag, it was pretty much full. I was able to get the rings you wanted but there was no way anything else was going to fit," she held out a small crystal globe with a large wolf in midstride inside. "Except for this, I saw it under one of the tables and when I saw what it was… Well I couldn't resist. It's so cute!"

The wolf looked anything but cute. It was a large white beast with a massive muscled hump across its back and large sharp teeth. Blood red eyes seemed to convey a sense of angry intelligence.

"Isn't he just awesome?" she said as she hugged the crystal to her chest and then gave it a quick kiss.

To their amazement, the moment her lips touched the crystal egg it cracked open with a pop. The little wolf shook itself free of the crystal dust and quickly leapt from the cracked crystal egg to Joslyn's shoulder. It began nuzzling her neck and howling softly as the kids sat in stunned amazement.

Indy caught a glimpse of the broken shell and picked it up to look a little closer at it. "I've seen this stuff before. Doc had shards of it all over his chest when he was in the hospital and that flash reminded me of something else. I saw a flash just like that when the SEALs had us tied up on that boat. The bag they had must have been full of those things."

"So where did they all come from," Joslyn asked as she hugged the small wolf tight to her chest. "We didn't see anything like that in the storage room."

"I don't remember seeing them either," Jon said. "And I went through pretty much everything in the room when you guys were play fighting."

"I'm guessing Doc has a secret stash of artifacts hidden somewhere in that plant," Indy said thoughtfully." Now that we know what we are looking for and with that telescope, we have a way to find it. Let's go back, grab something to eat and then come back here to set up our stakeout."

The Razor was nearly invisible to the hydro plant as it sat hidden in the trees. Joslyn was busy playing with the white wolf, so Indy and Jon took turns staring through the telescope at the distant building. They used the artifact to search the building room by room. Many of the rooms in the building held equipment vital to the buildings original purpose and a few others were just empty office space. But after a bit of searching they did find several very important rooms. The armoury had two guards stationed near a thick metal door. Inside the room, there were rows of weapons and armour lining the walls.

The next bunch of rooms they found were set up as a small prison block. Three navy SEALs were in one room and three Chinese Special Forces were in another. Indy thought it was a little strange that these rooms had less of a guard than the armoury. Only one person stood guarding this area although it appeared he was well armed. He was equipped with artifact armour and a static whip.

The last important room they came across was Doc Hocking's lab. Freshly rebuilt, the room was large and heavily fortified. No guards were stationed at this large metal door and Indy doubted anyone needed to. Instead of continuing a room-by-room search for the doctor, Jon suggested to leave the telescope dialled in to the lab. So they sat there in the dark shade of the trees and waited for Doc to show.

In the back seat, the wolf began to pace and growl softly. Jon was just opening his mouth to say something when they heard a noise coming up from behind them.

Thrump thrum thrumpt. Two sleek black shapes streaked by overhead. Above them, the sleds could barely be seen through the thick canopy of leaves. The two APGs banked hard and accelerated to the top of the hydro plant where they disappeared from view.

Indy was trying to scan the rooftop with the telescope but he was frustrated with the dials and handed the artifact over to Jon. "See if you can get this damn thing to work."

Jon took hold of the artifact and dialled in the proper settings. Within seconds, he was giving them a running commentary on what was happening on the roof. "Two guys in black suits just landed on the roof. They aren't taking their helmets off so I can't be sure who they are but one of them is pretty big. I am guessing it's probably Zeus. Maybe Doc is the other driver. Anyway, they are heading downstairs. I will try to pick them up on the next floor."

Jon redialled the telescope and put it back up to his eye. "It looks like the men in black are heading towards the prison wing."

"That's weird," Jon said. "They still have their helmets on. Anyway, they are almost at the first door now... wait! The big one just decked the guard. Ouch, the guard is down and out cold, the other guy just pulled a gun. He got the drop on a second guard that was inside the rooms. Hang on, that's no guard. Indy... your dad is in there."

Indy felt his heart freeze in his chest. "What's going on in there?"

Jon took up the artifact again and re-focused on the prison wing. "You dad has his hands up and they are walking him to the cells. They are opening up all the doors. Both the SEAL team and Special Forces are out. It looks like they are all yelling and waving their hands around at your dad. Daniel is just shaking his head, he has something in his hand. I can't tell what it is... it's too small. Looks like a jewellery box or something. Ohhh... Zeus just ripped it out of his hands. Now they are shoving him into the cell."

"No!" Jon screamed.

"What happened?" Indy demanded.

Jon turned to look at his friend, his face had gone pale, and he dropped his eyes. "They just shot your dad."

Indy was out of the ATV in a flash, grabbing the ring artifact and the chameleon cloak from a startled Joslyn. The little wolf gave a growl of irritation but stayed curled up on her lap.

"You guys wait here. Call me on my cell once I get to the rooftop. You can guide me in from there," Indy said and then ran off at a full sprint, not waiting for a reply.

The chameleon cloak works best when standing still but Indy hoped it would help hide him enough to blend in and slip past any guards. He pulled his Bluetooth earpiece from his pocket and put it in his ear. With any luck, he could dodge any patrols on the ground and make it to the roof undetected. The horned ring in his hand spit out its white rope with a splat as he got to the wall. It was a perfect shot and the rope had stuck to the wall just a few feet from an upper story window. His earpiece chimed and when he answered Joslyn's soft voice filled his ear.

"Nice shot," she said. "You got a clear run to the roof. We haven't seen any of the patrols come by since the AGPs got to the roof."

"Thanks," Indy said abruptly. "Is my dad ok, is he still moving?" Indy was angry and he knew he wasn't thinking this through but he needed to get in there right now. If anyone had a chance to save his dad, he did. Indy pulled the horns of the rings together and he shot up the side of the building with incredible speed. After swinging himself onto the window ledge, Indy burst through the window. On the other side of the glass was just an empty office room. He was through the small room and moving to the prison wing before he got his next update.

"You just missed the men in black. They are on the roof getting into the AGPs."

"My dad?" Indy asked

"Indy… there's a lot of blood, but he is still moving. They dragged him into one of the cells and left him. He's ripping up bedding to bandage his leg right now. I think he will be ok."

"Is there anyone else in my way?" Indy demanded. Not that they would have stopped him he thought to himself.

"Nope. Jon says the guard is still KO'd and it looks like the SEALs and the Special Forces have left the building through a side door."

"Ok. Thanks Joslyn. Watch which way the AGPs go and tell Jon to keep an eye on those soldiers. I don't know what the hell they are up to, but it can't be good."

Indy ran past the security guard lying face down on the floor. He was at the cell doors only seconds later. This area of the building was mostly cement and metal. Even the carpeting was a dull grey in this section. Four heavy metal doors stood in a row along one side of the hallway. Three of them were wide open and a trail of blood led into the fourth. Indy tried the handle first, but the door was locked tight. A keypad controlled the locks on each of the prison doors.

He hammered on the door with his fists. Each punch echoed loudly in the stillness of the prison wing.

"Dad! Dad! Are you ok...? It's Indy. Can you hear me?"

"Relax son. I can hear you. I'm ok, how did you find me? Who told you I was down here?"

"I... Uh... Never mind dad, do you know the code for the door."

"The guards are the only ones with the codes. Go see if Sam is okay, he's the guard you passed in the hall. Zeus hit him pretty hard but if you can wake him up, he can get this door open."

Indy ran back to the guard and checked him over. A large lump at the back of his head showed where Zeus had hit him. There was blood flowing slowly from the man's nose as well.

He must have hit the floor hard when he went down. Indy checked his pulse and his breathing. The man was still alive, but wasn't responding to Indy's voice.

Indy ran back to his father's door. "I can't wake him dad." Indy kicked at the door in frustration.

"Don't bother trying to break in. We made sure that these doors were strong enough to hold those soldiers tight. Go call James and tell him what is going on. Make sure you tell him Zeus has the key to the tower. He'll know what you mean."

"Ok dad. Stay here…" Indy paused and thought about rephrasing that. "I mean I will be right back." Indy turned to run back to the guard station but a figure had come up behind him and was standing only a few feet away. It was Doc Hocking. The old man was wearing his usual attire, a white lab coat.

"Doc," Indy sneered. "You're gonna pay for this old man." Indy balled his fists and stepped toward the doctor. He didn't care how old the man was he was gonna make him pay for shooting his father.

A small black blur launched itself from just behind the Doc and hit Indy's knees like a cannon ball. Indy bounced once as his body hit the floor and skidded to a stop at Doc Hockings feet. Looking back Indy saw the little Minotaur crouched on the floor behind him. The little bull man was shaking its head as if trying to shake off dizziness. It abruptly sat down and closed its eyes.

When Indy looked back, he found Doc Hocking looming over him. Then the Doc did something that surprised Indy. He reached down to help him stand.

"I know you don't like me junior. Your father and I have had our differences but I want you to know I didn't do this. I

171

would never do anything like this to anyone, least of all, your father. I respect the man way too much for that."

"If you didn't do this then who did? There is no way Zeus thought this all up by himself."

"I believe Zeus is just the muscle in this scenario. My team have been…let's say… keeping an eye on the man for a while now. We also believe that a man by the name of Colonel Tapper is involved in this whole mess. After some digging into Zeus's background, we found out that the good Colonel was a Commander of a Navy SEAL team in the early 1990's. By strange coincidence, your friend Zeus was a member of that very same team. The other SEALs were probably taking their orders from Colonel Tapper as well. To what end I can't be sure of. I am assuming that they were after a weapon of some sorts but I still haven't figured exactly what."

Indy nodded his head as he put the pieces together. Tapper and Zeus, Zeus and the SEALs. Zeus was probably feeding them information the whole time.

"But what changed? Indy thought to himself. "Why were they making their move now? Maybe it was something to do with the key his father had spoken about." His thoughts shifted back to his father.

"Doc, we need to get my father out of that room. He's been shot and bleeding pretty bad," Indy said as he looked over at the imposing metal door.

"Yes, yes, I know. I have several of my team watching Zeus and when they showed up here they told me right away."

Doc walked up to the metal prison door and tapped lightly. "Mr. Locke, stand back from the door. I brought a little bit of something that should get us through that door in no time."

Doc Hocking unslung a heavy backpack from his shoulder and retrieved a large plastic bottle from its depths. He uncapped the bottle and started pouring its watery contents over the hinges and locks of the door. The result was instantaneous. Smoke started to billow out from wherever the liquid was poured.

Doc called out to Daniel Locke Sr. "Try not to breathe any of the smoke in. It wouldn't be very good for you," he took his own advice and backed away from the smoking door.

On his way, he scooped the dazed Minotaur off the floor.

"Just a minute longer. Ok. Go ahead junior. You should be able to knock that door down now."

Indy ran at the door full speed and crashed through knocking the door down as he barrelled into the room. His father was sitting on a cot at the rear of the room with his shirt pulled over his mouth. Blood was seeping through a piece of cloth that had been wrapped around his leg.

Indy ran to his dad and hugged him close.

The doctor followed him into the room. "Ahem," he cleared his throat. "I am assuming Zeus has the key to the tower now?"

"Yeah. They came storming in here as I was relaying a message to the SEAL team. They shot me in the leg and took..." Daniel hesitated looking from his son to the doctor. "They took the panda."

This news clearly frustrated the doctor. "I told you not to keep that thing in plain sight. Too many people saw it during the SEAL attack in the op room. I am sure it didn't take long for someone to figure out the wish box wouldn't work without it. I warned you to leave it with me but you didn't listen to me... again."

"Now is not the time Doc. We need to send your team in and take Zeus out before he can make a mess of things."

"That may be a problem. The science team is currently engaging the soldiers in the armoury. It appears that Zeus has created sufficient distractions that will occupy them for the time being."

The Doc looked at Indy and raised an eyebrow. "Your son and his... friends, might be able to slow Zeus down enough to enable the armoured units to move in and take him out.

"Indy? I know he has been brave lately but there is no way I am sending him up against Zeus. I know what that man is capable of."

Indy watched quietly as the Doc motioned for him to come closer.

"Daniel... I know you think I have been keeping secrets from you lately and you are right. We can discuss that later. I also kept some details from you in regards to your son. Trust me I wanted to tell you the moment I found out but I promised your son I would keep his secrets"

Daniel Locke senior was stunned. He turned to regard his son with a dazed expression on his face. "Why would you want to keep anything from me? What could be so bad that you couldn't tell me? I would have understood. Your mother would have understood."

"Dad... I... I... I don't know why I didn't tell you. I guess it was just nice to know you thought I was a hero. It's been so long since we have all been together and then it was one thing after the other that kept us apart. Between this whole aurora thing, mom healing people and you dealing with the United States and then the United Nations. I really didn't want to bother you or mom. When mom… left, well it was too late to tell you then. One more thing on your plate and I think you might have had a nervous breakdown." Indy had a hard time looking into his father's eyes. He knew he had let him down but, done was done.

Daniel Locke was staring at his son but his shoulders had slumped slightly and his eyes seemed to lose some of their natural sparkle.

"I'm so sorry junior. I know I have been busy, I was only trying to make sure everyone was safe. I promise I will make it up to you."

"Dad, you don't have to worry about it. I understand. I should have told you everything but I never found the right time."

Doc Hocking cleared his throat. "We are out of time, could we just show your father your ability, so we can move on.

Indy nodded and stepped back from his father. He lifted his shirt to reveal the swirling black dragon tattoo. Lately he could feel exactly where on his skin the tattoo was, just by the heat of it.

This tattoo is an artifact from some of grandpa's stuff you had me bring in," Indy said. "With it, nothing can hurt me. Nothing can cut me or shoot me. I can't even drown. I jumped down the cliffs to the beach and landed without a scratch."

Daniel Locke senior reached out his hand to his son's chest. The dragon tattoo there swirled and danced around his father's touch but finally relented and settled under his hand.

"Its amazing Indy. I really wish you would have told me." His dad started laughing. "You are bulletproof? Is it really true? I can't believe it, that's awesome."

"Ok, Indy," Doc said. "Your friends are waiting for you outside. They have been putting those artifacts you borrowed to good use." The old man winked at him with a knowing look and then smiled. "I noticed several Items were missing from the experiments room earlier. Your friends did an excellent job of moving things around to cover their absence but they forgot one thing."

Indy's mouth dropped open. He was so busted.

The doctor continued. "They forgot that even though the leather cloak is invisible, it still casts a shadow. The cameras on the ceiling were able to pick up a slight shadow on the floor wherever Ms. McCloud walked. It was a brilliant manoeuvre though and I believe it has worked out in all our favour."

"Indy, get to the tower and warn Hank. He might be able to help," Daniel said. "Try to get my panda away from him if you can and above all else make sure you keep your friends safe."

"The science team will meet you there as soon as they deal with the soldiers. Doc added as he patted Indy on the shoulder."

Indy nodded and ran from the room. There was no way he was going to let his father down. It was time for a little payback.

EDEN 21 – GOING DOWN?

The Razor ripped through the underbrush moving fast. The gang were strapped in tight and Joslyn was driving hard. As the trees cleared and they found the Appleton road dead ahead. They bounced onto it and were at Hanks in no time flat.

As they pulled into the lot, they could see two sleek shapes parked just outside the shop. They climbed silently from the ATV. Jon raised the artifact telescope to his eyes and began fiddling with its odd bubble controls.

"I don't see anyone yet," he murmured. "Looks like the storage rooms are empty. I get some weird feedback from the lower one, some kind of interference."

"Try Hank's place," Joslyn said quietly.

Jon panned the telescope across to Hank's store and abruptly yelled. "Fire! The whole store is on fire. I can see Hank, it looks like he is hurt. He's on the floor just inside the front door."

Indy broke into a run heading towards the store. Without warning, the front of the store blew out in a rush of bright flames. Glass sprayed everywhere as the three kids were knocked to the ground from the force of the explosion.

"You guys ok?" Indy checked on his friends but they had just been knocked down and neither one had suffered any cuts from the flying glass. Indy was up and running towards the flames that were dancing on Hanks porch only seconds after he had fallen.

"Hank!" he found the old farmer crumpled on the floor just feet from the door. Luckily, the explosion only blew out the windows and left Hank in one piece.

"I... Got... Si... Help," Hanks gravelly voice stuttered and failed. "Don't worry big guy," Indy said. "I gotcha." Indy dragged the big man outside and once they were outside, Jon was there to help him. "Joslyn grab the first aid kit. Jon, go grab the artifacts."

When Joslyn came back from the ATV, she kneeled by the farmer's side and opened the first aid kit. "Try to keep still Hank. We're here now. You're gonna be alright," she said as she started cleaning his cuts and mopping up the blood.

"Stay with Hank," Indy told her. "He needs you. We got this."

They nodded at each other as Indy and Jon ran for the sinkhole. When they got there, they peered down into the hole. The pit was dark and silent below them. The generator inside Hanks store was probably destroyed in the explosion and the lights from the room below were all out.

"I'll go down first, hand me the rings," Indy said as he swung his legs out over the edge of the hole.

He took the rings from Jon and squeezed them tight. A ropy white mass fired off into the orchard hitting a tree with a splat.

He pulled out several more feet of the rope from the ring before sliding down into the hole.

"Ok I'm down," he whispered back up at Jon.

Jon slipped down the white silk rope and landed softly beside him. They could see light in the stairwell coming from the lower level. Jon pulled his sword from its scabbard and followed Indy down.

The lower level hummed with power but the only thing remaining in the room was the white box at the center of the room. All the racks and artifacts had been stripped from the room. They looked around the room and even inside the box but there was no one there.

"Indy, look at the wall," Jon whispered.

Two lights raced around the border of the wall where there was only one light before. The two lights raced back and forth across lines connecting the symbols together. A second symbol was now lit with a bright blue light.

Which symbol is it? Jon asked as Indy walked over to look at the glowing symbols on the wall.

"Valhalla," Indy said. "It's the one with the two swords. I wonder if it's another aurora or something else."

Jon followed Indy over to the wall and they stood side by side, looking at the pictograms.

Jon pointed at the Valhalla symbol. Look, it has the same circle ours does on the outside. That must be the aurora. I am guessing that the blue ball at the center must be the earth.

"But what would crossed swords mean," Indy asked. "Battle? War?"

"Nuclear war." The voice came from behind them and startled both kids.

Indy turned with surprise to see James standing there. Zeus was right behind him with Joslyn drape over one shoulder. Jon raised the Angel sword and moved to go after them but Indy held his friend back.

James sneered at Indy. "Thank you both for coming on such short notice. I was hoping you could make it to my little farewell party. It took a little planning and quite a bit of your father's money to put this all together. That and a few of the good doctor's baubles in the right pockets gave me everything I needed," he said. "You see, your father is a very short sighted man. He could not see the bigger picture. It is quite noble of him to want to save the world but when I said we needed to find the other places listed on these walls, he forbade me. He treated me like some kind of lap dog, incapable of any intelligent decisions. He would not even consider looking for these places. Your father acted as if his word was law and no one could convince him otherwise. I am sick of it... and him."

James started pacing the room and waving his gun around as he gestured. "I will show him. I will find each and every place listed on these walls. When I do, I am going to put your father in his place. I will put everyone in their place."

"My family trusted you," Indy said. "You are like a brother to me, how could you shoot my dad?"

"A funny choice of words there Indy." James laughed. "It seems that Daniel..." The wristwatch James was wearing buzzed. "Ah, it seems we are out of time. The valet is bringing my submarine around as we speak. Let's get on with it then, shall we?"

James nodded at Zeus. "Wake her up and put her over there next to the box," he then looked at Jon and Indy. "You two back up or someone here gets dead."

James had pulled a handgun from a holster under his arm. The black handgun aimed straight at Jon, so they did as they were told. Zeus dropped Joslyn next to Jon and then broke a small stick under her nose. Joslyn coughed and started to wake up. Indy and Jon reached down to help her up and they all stood together watching as Zeus returned to James's side.

"Indy." James said. "I'm really sorry it had to be this way. Trust me when I say I really don't want to hurt any of you. I swore an oath to your mom I would always watch out for you. After all, I watched you grow up. I taught you how to be a man when your father was too busy to be around. I know you might not believe me but your mother loved me and I loved her. When she died..."

"She's not dead," Indy interrupted.

A look of pity crossed James' face. "Anyway when we first found this room and this box we had no idea of its power. In fact, it took several days of work to determine what it does. But, in the end, it seems the simplest explanation is usually right. It's a wish box."

"Ya right," Indy laughed. "You really think I'm gonna believe that crap."

"After everything you have seen the last few months, you're not even going to give this a chance? Anyway you don't have to believe in it to make it work." James laughed harder. "You just have to say the words. After all you owe me one."

"How's that?" Indy asked.

James started pacing the floor across from them as he started to explain. "When we first came here and discovered these treasures, we discussed how we would bring them to a museum. Your father discovered the box under a tractor we had to remove from the room. He was leaning on that box when he said..."

"I wish I knew what this stuff was for. A light filled the air and the box vibrated and hummed below his hands. When it was done, we opened the lid and a little panda man popped out. That little fury abomination whispered something in your father's ear. As far as I know, it was the only time that damn panda ever spoke. He has never said another word."

Your father quickly made a few more wishes as he stood over the box. None of them activated the box again. It was a one shot deal. Your mom made the next wish. She said she wanted to heal all the world's ills. Again the box lit up and this time when it opened your mom's staff was inside."

"It was incredible, fantastic, and unbelievable all at once. We were awestruck and debated our next wish for hours as we stood hovering over the box. Ideas of money, fame, glory, and knowledge were kicked around. Finally, I decided that my wish would be for eternal life. However, before I could make my wish, your mother took me by the hand. If this is to be your one wish, she said, I want you to promise me you will take care of Indy... As long as you both live. At the time I had no idea how the oath would bind me to you."

"I swore my oath to your mother and then made my wish. The box lit up like before and when I opened it, I found a large round crystal pendant. One half was a white crystal tiger and the other, a black dragon. As I reached into the box a strange burning feeling filled my body and the crystal disappeared, along with this white box."

James lifted his shirt to show Indy his bare chest where a white tiger tattoo sat gazing back at them. The big cat moved just like his dragon tattoo.

"So you see." James said. "I know of your tattoo and your invulnerability. I know because I have the same gifts.

We are in this together Indy, you and I. My promise to your mom will protect you for the rest of my life."

He shook a finger at Indy. "But make no mistake. If you get in my way, I will destroy everything you cherish and your eternal life will be lived in torment. Now as for what we came here for in the first place. When we discovered the box again on this level, it would not activate for anyone. It took a while to figure out but in the end, we found the key. It seems the little panda man was more than just an instruction manual." James produced the ornate jewellery box from inside his jacket.

James pointed the gun at Jon. "Jon put your hands on the box and repeat my words exactly. If you do not do exactly what I say, I will shoot the girl. I want you to speak slowly and clearly. I will let you both go after we are done. I swear on my life."

"Repeat after me. I wish for a way for us to leave the aurora without crystalizing." James said.

Jon repeated slowly and the box lit under his fingers.

"Back, back, back." James shooed them away with gun and then lifted the lid. "Excellent work Jonathan."

James reached in to the box and brought out a golden-skinned apple. He smelled it and gave it a tap against his teeth.

"Fantastic," he said and tossed the apple at Joslyn who caught it effortlessly. "Take a bite of this. If I'm right, you will thank me for it."

Zeus walked back over to them and tapped Joslyn on the side of her head with the gun when she hesitated.

"Ok, ok," she said and took a small bite of the apple. It crunched loudly in the sudden quiet.

Indy's breath caught in his throat as the frost melted instantly from her face. Her frozen dead eye unclouded as it refocused on the apple.

Joslyn started crying in relief and collapsed to the floor.

"Zeus." James said. "The apple if you please."

The big man tore the bitten fruit from Joslyn's hand and pocketed it.

James ordered Zeus again. "Bring her over here and then grab the rest of these apples out of the box."

Zeus moved to obey as they watched silently.

"Same rules Ms. McCloud. Speak the words. No one dies. We all leave here happy."

James told her his next wish. "I wish for a compass to lead me to the other places named on these walls."

She repeated what he said exactly as he said it.

The box flashed again and when Zeus opened the lid, he pulled out a large metal disc. Glowing pictograms lined the outer edges of the bright golden metal.

"Very nice. Hand it here Zeus and then you may make the last wish." James commanded.

Zeus handed over the disk and practically ran over Joslyn as he rushed to make his wish.

"Remember." James scolded. "Don't get greedy." James tapped a little jewellery box tucked into the waist of his pants. "The little panda warned Daniel that the box could react badly if you wished for too much."

Zeus waved his hand in aggravation, clearly ignoring anything James had said.

Zeus placed his hand on the white box and thought for a short moment before making his wish. "I wish for long life, great strength, incredible knowledge and a weapon to kill my enemies."

James looked in horror at Zeus's arrogance. The room shook and the air vibrated but the box did not light. Instead, a circle around the base of the box formed and the rumbles stopped.

"My hands are stuck," Zeus cried out as he leaned away from the box.

The veins on his neck and arms popped as he tried to pull his hands free. In the next instant, the floor beneath the box disappeared. Zeus and the box dropped away into darkness.

They waited in silence to hear the box hit bottom. They waited and waited and waited until a soft sound came that was almost like the sound of rocks smashing. The hole in the floor rematerialized as they watched.

"Oh bother." James cursed. "Anyway, thank you all for the help. As I promised, I leave you all here unharmed. See you again sometime kids."

James smiled wickedly before he said. "Oh, on second thought. I think I should leave you with a little present."

He pulled two grenades from his pocket. "I really didn't want this to end this way, so messy."

"Indy the vines are... moving," Joslyn said as her eyes focused on the wall behind James.

A whine filled the room and the symbols on the walls started to glow brighter. A new, larger circle lit around each of them. The large circles began to swirl with color and the room around them started to shake. Suddenly they were all thrown to the ground as the room lurched. Wind rushed into the room from the stairwell. As the rumbling began to fade the circles on the walls sparked to life. They looked like windows.

Joslyn and Jon each turned to look and watched the valley spreading out below them through the odd swirling windows.

Jon walked over to the window and said. "We are not underground anymore guys. I can see the ocean through this one," Jon looked closer at the window. "Look," he said. This window has a symbol on it. It's almost invisible but I can still see the edges.

A dark shape flashed by Joslyn's window. "What the hell was that?" she screamed.

They looked around the room, finally noticing James was gone.

"I'm guessing that was James," Indy said softly.

"Indy you have to stop him," Joslyn told him. "Don't worry about us, we will be fine. Just go get that bastard. You can't let him get away with those apples and the compass. If he finds another cache full of artifacts, he could cause a lot of problems for everyone. You never know, the next place could have some serious weapons. Who knows what James is capable of? We didn't even see this coming."

"Just think of your father's plans," Jon reminded him. "There will be no peaceful healing sanctuary with the threat that James now holds over us."

"But what can I do?" Indy asked. "He's too strong for me and we have the exact same powers!"

Jon pulled the short angel sword from the scabbard across his back. "Back when we were at the experiment room Doc showed me something on this sword. I wasn't sure what he meant at the time but, well just watch."

Jon pulled at the high cross guard with one hand. It clicked loudly and the blade began to shimmer and hum. Blue electricity traced the blade as it hummed in the air.

"Doc told me that a day might come when a dragon must need slaying. Sounded a bit odd at the time but you know Doc, eh? In any case, Doc said this sword was the only thing that might have a chance. I think he was talking about you, like maybe he was worried you might go bad or something."

Indy shot Jon a dark look as he considered his friends words but nodded in understanding as he realized the trust Jon had in telling him about the sword. Indy looked closer at the sword Jon was holding. "Well I can remember Joslyn hitting me with it. I think that was the only time since all this started I have felt any kind of pain."

"Just don't cut yourself with it flyboy," Joslyn scolded but laughed quickly after.

Indy smiled weakly and took up the blade. It was like holding raw lightning in his palm. It crackled and spat as he held it high above his head.

"Tap the bottom of the hilt to turn it off," Jon told him.

Indy flicked the blade off and ran for the stairs. Joslyn and Jon followed. As they reached the top of the stairs, they found the view was radically different from the last time they were here.

The valley spread out below them on all sides. The room that had been here was gone, replaced by a flat floor with low walls and no ceiling.

Looking over the edge, they saw scattered debris and a portion of paved parking lot far down below.

"Well at least Hank isn't gonna be mad about the fire," Jon joked.

"Oh Jon," Joslyn grimaced.

"Wish me luck," Indy said as he stepped to the edge and placed his hands on the low wall.

"Remember..." Joslyn placed an arm around him and whispered in his ear. "Nothing can hurt you Indy. Not bullets and not even bombs. You can do this."

Indy nodded at her and gave her a quick hug before stepping away from her and the wall. He breathed in and out a few times before his resolve set it. Indy ran for the edge and leapt.

EDEN 22 – CRASH LANDINGS

The fall was over in the space of a few wild heartbeats. Dirt and grass exploded away from where he landed. This time he landed in a crouch instead of sprawled flat out. He would have gotten major style points for the landing if anyone had been watching. Indy took a deep breath of relief and was up and running for the sleds before the dust cleared. A large body was slumped over the only remaining sled. It was Hank.

"Hank? Hank, are you ok?" Indy asked.

The big man had blood streaming down his face and his eyes were almost swollen shut.

"Ahh. Indy," Hank tried to speak but the words came out slow and quiet. "I tried to stop him. But I couldn't. He just laughed at me when I hit him. It looked like he wanted to get away with both of these... things. I couldn't let him... get away with it... I saw what he did to... my store."

"I think he was about to shoot me when we heard you coming. He pretty much ran away after that."

"Where did he go Hank? Which way?" Indy asked as he looked around for James.

Hank gestured at the white tree in the distance as he rolled off the sled. "He went there."

Indy's mouth grimaced as he set the sword down into the gel. He quickly climbed in after it and turned the AGP on.

189

"Joslyn and Jon are stuck up there," he told Hank. "Call up to the castle and get some help. I'm going after James."

The AGP streaked up and away as Indy stretched full out. The ground blurred below him as he flew. Within seconds, he found James. He could see James just ahead of him weaving in and out of the trees. It looked like the man was trying to be sneaky and hide in the darker sections of the forest. Indy was flying a little higher than the trees when he banked hard and dove at James's back. Indy tugged the sword free from the gel and it sparked to life. James must have heard the sword because at the last second he swerved away. The slicing blade severed a tall pine instead. The hard impact of hitting the tree threatened to tear the blade from his hand as he passed. Indy decided to put the sword back into the gel before he dropped it. It took all his skill to concentrate on flying the sled and keep James in sight. He followed him closely dodging over and under branches and fallen trees. The bushes streaked below him as the forest fell away and the rocky ridgeline appeared. The sun was setting over the water ahead as the sleds neared the ocean blowholes.

Giant plumes of water rocketed up around them as the two sleds weaved in and out. Between the suns glare and the mist of the water, Indy had a hard time trying to track the other sled. He lost sight of it for a moment and by the time he found it again James was out over top the sandy beach.

The other sled shot out low over the water and came around in a slow turn. It was about to land on the beach where the land, sea, and aurora met. Indy saw a small boat paddling in as James landed his sled and began waving to the boat.

"I can do this," Indy thought to himself. Indy stretched out and dove. Something bright flashed by and the sled passed through a smoke trail. The smoke trailed back to the beach and the boat that had just come ashore. Three men in black fatigues stood in the sand aiming more rockets his way.

The rockets came at him in a steady stream as his AGP dodged left and right. Further, up the beach he could see James eating a gold apple and waving in his general direction. Several more rockets streaked by as Indy closed in on James, threatening to turn his ride into carbon dust. Indy was within a hundred feet as James finished the apple. The left over apple core was casually tossed over his shoulder as he waited for Indy to get closer.

Indy aimed straight at the man as he dove. The Angel sword sparked to life as he pulled it from the gel folds beside him. There was only him and James on the beach in that moment. James braced himself in a low stance, unafraid of the incoming AGP missile.

The ancient angel blade slashed down as Indy passed by overhead. Again, the blade tugged and almost dropped from his hand. Indy looked up as he passed by and realized his mistake too late. The aurora shimmered before him and he passed through it before he could alter his course. The cliffs beyond the aurora came up fast and crystal dust shattered in the air around him. Then there was only darkness.

Indy came to as someone was calling his name. Over and over, he heard it but the world around him remained dark to his eyes. He tried moving but everything hurt. Something in his chest throbbed and he couldn't feel his legs. The pain was unbearable.

Indy thought the voice grew louder as the darkness started to overwhelm him. Just before he passed out again he swore he could feel someone wrap him in a warm embrace.

EDEN 23 - CHOOSING FATES

When Indy woke again he was in a hospital bed. He looked around and realized he was back in the castle's hospital wing. The room was empty except for him. He was stiff all over and a groan slipped from his lips as he moved around on the bed. Gauze and bandages covered most of his body. His left leg was in a heavy cast and he could see numerous well-wishers had signed it. Pictures of hearts, dragons, angels, and xo's covered the long white cast.

"Awake now honey? Just lie back and relax." A tall woman with long red hair in a nurse's gown had appeared at his side out of thin air. "You aren't well enough to get out of bed just yet young man."

"Who are you?" Indy asked the older woman. He didn't remember ever seeing her in the castle before. Maybe he had hit his head harder then he thought.

"Don't worry about me right now, you have some other friends waiting patiently outside. They have been waiting for you quite a while now. I'll go get them."

The nurse or doctor swept from the room and moments later, his friends came bursting into the room.

"You're ok!" Jon yelled as he came running over.

Joslyn ran to his other side, silent except for tears streaming down her face. A worried smile creased her face.

193

"I'm a little sore but I think I will live," Indy said as he smiled up at his friends. He reached up to touch Joslyn's long blonde hair. He could feel the frost sticking to his fingers as he dropped his hand back to the bed.

"Your hair," he said.

Indy reached up again to brush Joslyn's frosted hair away from her face. Her pale skin was covered in frost...

"It came back when she went through the aurora to bring you back," Jon said.

"You did that for me?" Indy asked.

Joslyn nodded. "Of Couse I did, I was the one who ate the apple after all. It worked Indy. It really worked. I searched outside the aurora for you for almost half the night. We weren't even sure if you were still in one piece or if the crash had shattered your... statue," she held up a hand to her icy hair. "But this didn't happen then. It just started coming back yesterday. Your dad thinks the effects of the apple are only temporary."

"How long have I been out?" Indy asked worried about what he had missed.

His friends looked at each other and then back to him.

"You've been unconscious for almost two weeks Indy," Jon said.

"Two weeks? What about James? Did I kill him? What about the Chinese soldiers on the beach?" Indy asked in a rush.

Jon held up both hands. "Slow down dude. We aren't exactly sure what happened down there the cameras were out. We can only guess."

Jon pulled a backpack off his shoulder and rummaged through it. He pulled out a gold apple core, a large chunk of flattened metal and two pieces of black crystal.

Indy's heart sank as he reached for the broken dragon crystal. The crystal was cold and dead as he gripped it tightly to his chest.

The metal he recognized as a piece of the compass James had taken from the white box. He could see several different pictograms along one rounded edge.

"The sword must have gone right through his backpack. It took a nice big chunk out of this piece of metal compass though," Indy said with a half-smile. Too bad I don't see any of his blood on it."

"It turns out Sasser was keeping an eye on James for a while now. He had been collecting evidence against him when he uncovered the plot to sell us out to a bunch of Chinese mercenaries. I guess Sasser was waiting in your dad's office when the whole thing went down at the Hydro plant. James and Zeus must have gotten wind of it and decided to act."

"That's not the half of it either," Joslyn said. "We have some good news too. Sasser told me that the radio jamming stopped shortly after the escape. The United Nations had come to a collective international agreement that your dad supports fully. Boats have been coming in every day for the last week. Your dad and several other people have already started planning a new town out near the Appleton border."

"Ya, you must have seen some of the new volunteer nurses. They were some of the first people to come off the boats," Jon's face smiled widely as he looked around the room, maybe expecting to see one of the new nurses.

Joslyn elbowed him and continued. "The international agreement your dad signed, states that our little valley is now a

195

recognized country for as long as the aurora surrounds us. Your dad has decided to call it Eden. Just like in the tower's pictograms. In the meantime your dad is accepting a limited number of citizen's, he is putting preferential treatment to those who are sick or dying."

Indy was blown away by so much good news. He slumped back down on the bed as he tried to wrap his head around it all. Eden? A new country? New citizens? It was all a little hard to believe.

"Wait… you said he was letting in people that are sick and dying? You mean Eden is healing people again?"

His friends looked down at their feet for a moment.

Joslyn started to cry again and Jon moved to put an arm around her. "Indy I don't know how to tell you this but… we think you were dead, at least for a few minutes," he said with the gravest expression on his face. "By the time a helicopter got us down from the tower and we found you… Well it was too late to do too much. But as soon as Joslyn dragged you back through the aurora, your heart started again. You were barely breathing but you were still with us."

Joslyn's eyes were filled with tears. "When your dad found out what happened he was devastated. I've never seen such pain and grief in one person's eyes. But then something inside him snapped. He vowed to nurse you back to health no matter what he had to do. He prayed for you every night underneath your mom's tree."

"Then about two days after we brought you back…" the tree started to bloom. The flowers that came out were so beautiful. Something changed about this valley that day, something in the air. It was as if all the energy had come back again. It reminded me of the time I touched the staff, and I mean every single one of us felt it. From that very day on we noticed that cuts were beginning to heal faster than normal."

"But I died? How can anything bring back someone from the dead? How is that even possible?"

"Indy," Joslyn said as she reached for his hand. "Your dad had a couple of theories about that. He guessed that you might have only just stopped breathing when I had found you. The shock of passing through the aurora again probably kick started your heart. You have to understand what shape you were in. It's a miracle you weren't killed instantly when you crashed. I think your dragon saved you, you must have hit the cliff before its power drained away. Doc said that it also saved you from being crystalized or frost scarred. Eden heals us slowly now. It's not like when your mom was able to just wave her staff and boom you're healed."

"Your dad made several deals with different countries after the UN deal and had specialists flown in. A couple of the hospital rooms were converted to surgery units and a bunch of medical equipment was installed."

It is pretty cool to see your dad in action. He has a bunch of people that are helping out, kinda like a council. Every country willing to aid us and protect us has been given a seat and a voice on the council. Just like the United Nations."

"So he finally got his wish," Indy said. "I'm proud of him, where is he?"

"We called him as soon as the nurse told us you were awake," Jon said.

As if summoned his father strode through the hospital doors. His eyes were bright and clear as he embraced his son

197

gently. "It looks like you are feeling better, is there any lingering pain?"

"Nope, I feel great dad. No aches, no pains, but this cast is a little itchy."

"Good to hear junior. We can get that taken care of right away. Thank heavens you're awake. You had me so worried. I need you now more than ever."

"What's wrong dad? What's happened?" Indy asked, fear growing in the pit of his stomach as he watched the expression on his father's face change.

Pain and anguished flickered in his father's eyes while Indy lay helpless on the hospital bed.

After a long silent minute his father spoke. "I haven't been very honest with you Indy."

"About what?" Indy asked.

"It's kind of hard to explain but here goes. Your friends filled me in about what happened in the tower and all about James and what he told you. I need to tell you that..."

"If you are about to tell me James is my real father, I will freak out."

"No Daniel, you are my son. Please stop interrupting me, you're just like your mom."

Indy let out a sigh of relief and nodded for his dad to continue.

Daniel senior looked sceptically at his son before he spoke. "Your friends told me about everything, including this. He poked a finger at the broken dragon lying on Indy's chest. Anyway what's done is done from now on I want the truth from you, no secrets."

Indy nodded his head and gave his father a half smile.

"In return, I am going to be more open with you too. The first thing I want to show you is this. Daniel pulled a small jewellery box from inside his shirt."

"Is that the...You got him back? How...?" his father looked at him hard and Indy stopped talking.

"My little friend came back today, this morning in fact. When I woke up, the jewellery box and the panda man were sitting on my nightstand. I don't know how, no one came into my rooms, but there he was. There is something very special about this little creature. It can do some very incredible things, if we are lucky... he might do us a little favour right now"

As if summoned the little jewellery box opened and the panda man popped out and jumped down on to Indy's chest. It looked around the room at the humans looking down on it and smiled briefly. It noticed the broken dragon lying not far from it, and it walked over. The panda made an odd humming noise as it rubbed its hands over the broken edges of the dragon. With a soft sucking noise, the dragon blurred together and became whole again. Satisfied the panda back flipped away and then cannonballed back into its box.

It waved at its audience and then slammed the jewellery box lid shut.

The black dragon gleamed atop Indy's chest as they all stood watching it in stunned silence. Indy reached his hand out to the dragon crystal and stopped just an inch away. Indy looked from the dragon to his father and then at his friends.

His father smiled back at him and said. "You have a choice this time. At least now, you know how things work. But, I'm afraid that I might influence your choice. I am sorry. While you were unconscious, the tower... changed. I know you probably didn't get a good look at it. It's confusing but let me try to explain. On one side of the tower is a large door and inside is a young boy named Adam. Adam has told us that a great evil will be unleashed upon this world tonight at midnight. He said that the tower cannot contain it any longer and that this evil grows stronger every day. If that evil breaks free of the tower's imprisonment, our whole world will be in jeopardy. He said that to stop this evil from coming forth, a guardian must be chosen, to venture forth and defeat this evil."

"That sounds a bit over dramatic," Indy said trying to lighten the mood but the smiles he hoped for did not appear. If anything, their faces grew even more grim.

"Those are his words, not mine. He has also imposed several rules on us," Daniel continued. "To become the tower guardian you must submit to a series of tests. Adam only allows one single attempt at this test though. Everyone in the valley has given it a shot and everyone who has tried has failed."

"From what I understand, Warren Hocking was the closest so far, when the tower spit him out he said he was about half way up," Jon added with a sour expression.

"Spit him out?" Indy asked.

"Yeah..." Joslyn said. "As soon as you fail or if you get too injured to continue, it kicks you out. A hole just appears in the floor and whoosh, out you go. It's like a big water slide, without the water."

Jon and Joslyn exchanged looks and started laughing uncontrollably.

"What's so funny?" Indy asked.

"Warren," Jon said. "When we found him he was covered head to toe in some kind of spider's web."

"Nobody knows for sure how long he was out there." Joslyn said through a small giggle. "He was stuck to the ground head first at the base of the tower. If Doc hadn't of been so worried about him and waited around so long, it might have been days before anyone found him."

"Oh, by the way, Allen wanted me to give you a message," Jon said. "He said to tell you that Karma is his new best friend."

Indy smiled at the thought of the little spiders spewing out of a broken silver artifact in Warren's pocket. Indeed Karma was a friend.

"So what exactly is in the tower? What kind of tests or challenges are in there?" Indy asked, growing very curious.

"We aren't allowed to tell you. Adam said if anyone does, then that person wouldn't be allowed in. He knows too, Allen told me all about his test and now Adam won't let me in," Jon said, his voice layered with guilt.

"There isn't much time Indy." His father said gently. "Tonight is the last night. There is no one left inside the valley willing or able to try."

Daniel Locke reached out for his son's shoulder.

"It's a great burden, son. Your friends have told me about the tattoo and I know about the headaches, black outs and the loss of… some of your senses." His father's eyes flickered to Joslyn and back. "But we need your help. I think… I know you are the only one that can do this," he patted the little jewellery box as he spoke. "In the end all our lives are in your hands."

Daniel Locke looked at his son and smiled. "I love you, no matter what you choose. I have asked everyone to stay inside the castle tonight… should the worst occur it may provide us with a small measure of protection," he bent down to kiss Indy on the forehead before leaving the room.

Joslyn and Jon had their eyes down or looking anywhere but at him. "We didn't know about the headaches and stuff," Jon said.

"I didn't want anyone to worry about me, there was so many other things going on," Indy smiled at Jon and thumped him in the arm.

Jon smiled back and wacked Indy's cast.

As Indy was howling in pain, Jon started to walk out the door. "I had to get that one in while I still could," he said and Indy listened to his friend's laughter fading into the next room.

Then only Joslyn and Indy were left in the room. They stared at each other for an eternity before she asked. "You remember our first kiss?" her voice faltered... "Could you even feel my lips or the heat of my face against yours?"

Indy couldn't speak so he just shook his head. He closed his eyes to hide the pain that pulsed through his heart, knowing how much she hurt inside just now.

The sweet smell of strawberries filled his nose as Joslyn leaned close. He felt the bed shift below him an instant before he felt warm soft lips on his. He could feel warm tear drops on his face moments before he could taste their saltiness in his mouth. The tears mixed with their kiss as her hand gripped his tightly. Her kiss seemed to linger on his mouth as a familiar tingling swept through his body. The smell of strawberries faded slightly at first followed by the soft touch of her hand. He knew at that instant the feeling of her kiss and the salt of her tears were the last things he might ever feel.

He opened his eyes to see her face pressed close, still kissing him. She must have sensed the changed because she pulled away quickly. She winked at him as she brushed her tears away. "Seeya later fly boy. Go save the world," Joslyn turned and ran from the room.

Indy watched as she ran from the room. When the doors had closed behind her, he looked down at his chest. His hand lay over the spot where the black dragon had been. Joslyn had placed his hand on the crystal dragon in mid kiss. She must have realized the choice was something he could not make on his own. It was an easy way out for him.

EDEN 24 – ADAM'S TOWER

Indy stood in the fading twilight staring at the massive tower in the middle of the vast orchard. The door at the base of the tower was open and light from inside spilled out onto the soft green grass surrounding it.

A voice called out to him as he advanced towards the opening. The voice was neither male nor female, and there was no telling how old it was either. It sang to him, soft and gentle in the night air. It called to him and guided him into the light.

When Indy stepped through the door the hairs on his arms raised and his flesh became spotted with goose bumps. The base of the tower was fairly wide and the single room inside was almost the same circumference as the tower itself. The soft flicker of candles burned throughout the room, illuminating bookshelves, and cabinets. The room contained no artwork on the walls but several hanging tapestries. Each tapestry was dark and difficult to look at, the flickering candle light not quite touching their surfaces. Every time he tried to look at one, he felt his eyes slide away. A singsong voice called to him again but this time Indy could make out the words. It was a welcome. At the far end of the room from the door was a little man dressed in a three-piece suit. Blonde curly locks flowed shoulder length around his pale angelic face. Piercing blue eyes told of an intelligence that far surpassed his youthful appearance. He sat waiting for Indy in a tall white chair and studying Indy's ever step. Indy came to a stop a few feet away as the little man held up his hand.

"Welcome Indy, I was hoping you would wake in time. You know, you gave us all a terrible fright. I want you to know how sorry I am you were injured. If you had managed to stay inside the influence of this tower, I can assure you would have come to no harm. But alas I rarely affect the outside world, no matter how much I wish to."

The angelic face smiled again and he held out a hand. "My name is Adam," he said.

Indy grasped the little man's hand and could feel the heat and soft flesh grip his own in a firm handshake. The heat startled Indy and he quickly let go of the little hand. It was the same dull heat that he felt when he touched his own dragon tattoo. Adams blue eyes twinkled in the candle light and the smile seemed to grow even wider on his chubby face.

"I'm sure you have questions my friend, but I am not here to answer them," Adam said and the smile slowly disappeared. "I really hate not telling you ever thing you wish to know, I am but a tool designed for a specific purpose. I have very strict rules that I must abide by," Adam looked side to side and then leaned forward. "I can however... confirm a few things you may already know," he said conspiratorially.

Indy leaned forward eager to learn anything that might solve the mysteries of the last month.

"The purpose of this tower is to protect the earth and the intelligent species that dwell upon it. As you have already figured out there are six towers. Each one of them has a specific purpose. All of them are designed to allow an intelligent race to expand and grow in relative safety. Free to live and learn on its own but the towers are put in place to protect that race from itself and other outside influences. These towers are only tools, when you come right down to it and a tool is only as useful as the person holding it. In the wrong hands, a tower becomes useless and unable to fulfill its purpose. When used properly the tower is not but a safeguard."

Indy was confused and amazed at the same time. "So my mother was right. Eden was created to solve the world's ecological problems."

Adam smiled at him again. "Your mother is a beautiful and intelligent woman. With her help, that tree will become this world's saving grace. But that tree is just a symbol of things to come. Humans can still choose to ignore the true meaning behind it and continue to pollute and destroy this planet."

"Will the tree die if the aurora fails?" Indy asked.

Adam looked sad again. His features seemed to droop and his smile faded. He did not answer.

"What can I do?" Indy asked. "If this tower is designed to save us there must be something I can do to make sure that happens."

The smile returned in an instant and Adam jumped down from his tall chair.

"In a perfect world no one would ever learn of these towers. But there have been rare instances where more than one tower becomes activated at a time. This activation causes a drain on the system that powers each tower. As a default setting, one of the towers assumes precedence, or in simpler

THE TOWER OF EDEN

terms becomes alpha. The alpha tower claims the majority of power during activation in some cases may cause any other active tower to shut down. It all depends on immediate need. Currently two towers are active. Eden, the one that we are in now and a second tower you may refer to as the Valhalla tower. You know the basic purpose of this tower but Valhalla has a much different purpose."

"James said something about nuclear war. Is that Valhalla's purpose, to prevent war?"

Again, Adam looked sad. He shook his head. "It will always be the choice of humans to do as they will. In this case, the tower will not prevent a war. One of its designs is to protect a small group of people from any and all outside interference. Like I said before each tower has a purpose and that purpose is to protect an intelligent species from extinction. More specifically it protects the people that control the tower."

Indy was dismayed. More questions began to fill his head and he didn't know how to begin asking Adam for the answers. Adam saved him the trouble.

"You have become distracted by our talk and I must remind you of your purpose here tonight," he said softly. "At the top of this tower is a room that controls the power flow to this region. Something in that room has interfered with this tower's operation. Normally with only one tower in operation, this wouldn't be a problem. But because there are multiple towers a cap is placed on the amount each tower generates."

"In order to maintain our energy aurora the power flow must be restored. Normally this duty would fall to me but given the current situation, safety protocols restrict me from entering that room and so a guardian must be called on for that duty. I have to warn you of one other thing. Inside the control room is a creature born of corruption that is currently being contained. If the tower powers down, that evil will be released upon the world. Let me be very clear. This creature will exist outside of this tower's effects and once free will threaten the lives of everyone on the planet."

Indy stood in shocked silence as he looked at Adam. "Why me? What makes me so special?"

"I have been watching you for some time now. You have all the necessary attributes a guardian needs. That job now falls on your shoulders, like it or not, I have chosen you for this honour. Normally you would be required to pass certain tests, but you already possess the guardian's symbol," Adam pointed at one of Indy's hands.

Indy looked down at his hand where the dragon had been sitting, wrapped around one wrist. The black tattoo was glowing with a familiar blue light.

"If you fail to reach the control room or choose to do nothing, this tower will power down the aurora in order to conserve power until control is re-established. Once the other tower has fulfilled its purpose this one tower shall reactivate, if the need for it still exists. Unfortunately everything we have begun here will be... undone."

"What about the people out there? What will happen to them if this tower shuts down?" Indy already knew the answer and Adam only confirmed it with another headshake.

"The people around this tower that have been affected by the aurora will become statues until this tower activates again. Under better circumstances, there are ways to transition them all safely. Those methods are not available at this time. You are starting to run out of time Indy. If you want this tower to remain active you should start on your journey now."

Indy nodded. "Ok. I am ready, where do I start."

"That is the hard part," Adam said. "The way this tower was built was to limit access to the control floor. Only one that has certain qualities and strengths will be able to get up there. Again, it may sound a bit convoluted but it is a safety protocol."

Adam pointed to a small bowl of red apples on a table beside him. "Take a bite from one of these apples. It will help you see... things differently."

Indy reached out to take an apple but paused when he noticed that the bowl was made of white wood with black snakes painted on its sides.

Something about the snakes made him uneasy. Hesitantly he reached his hand into the bowl and plucked out one of the red apples. He glanced up at Adam as he bit into the ripe fruit. Adam watched silently as Indy closed his eyes and swallowed the sweet fruit.

When he opened his eyes, the room had changed. It took a minute for him to focus his blurry eyes. A blue haze had settled over everything in the room. The tapestries he had noticed earlier were clear to him now. They all showed epic battles. Man fighting man, demons, and alien looking beasts. A couple others showed extreme natural disasters, floods, storms and volcanoes that blotted out the sun.

Adam cleared his throat softly and Indy turned back to look. Adam was gone, instead his sweet singsong voice echoed from somewhere ahead of him.

"Behind the tapestry on your left is the first door. As you go up the tower there will be six challenges. Master each challenge and the door to the control room will unlock. I wish you luck Daniel Locke junior. This is not an easy task I have set before you. Once you leave this room, you may not enter it again. You are not allowed to speak of the challenges and anything you hear or see in this tower once you begin. There are severe consequences in some cases, if you break these rules."

"Ok I understand, but where did you go?" Indy was confused and felt slightly dizzy.

"Do not fear my friend, I am with you." A disembodied voice called out.

Indy nodded at the empty air. It was just another of the many odd things that had happened to him in the last few weeks. He was beginning to expect things like this.

"Hey Adam, are you sure you can't just fix this control box for us? You know, save us all the trouble of going through these challenges," Indy asked quite seriously.

The air around him filled with laughter. A rich belly laugh reverberated through the tower. "In all my time I have never been asked a question like that. I will not short cut your task. Sometimes life is about the journey rather than the destination. I like you Indy. I wish I could say more but I cannot. One last thing to remember before you start your quest. The universe is all about balance. The same is true here. No matter what you do or do not do, your actions cause ripples around you. The bigger the ripple, the bigger the reaction. You might think of it as cause and effect."

"A word of warning, you must not pass through any black swirling portals. You simply are not ready to see what lies beyond. Your quest would be forgotten, at the very least and that would be disaster enough. Hurry now, good luck and fare well," Adam's singsong voice faded and the room grew silent.

Indy nodded his head again and stepped over to the tapestry. The large piece of artwork featured a large white tree with golden apples. Around the tree was a lake being fed by four rivers. Each river seemed to flow like molten silver. Indy lifted the tapestry and walked through an archway hidden behind it.

EDEN 25 – THE WHITE TREE

Inside the archway was a stairwell that rose up along the curving wall. Indy followed it until he came to a large door with a tree carved deep in the thick wood. Indy pushed the door open and stepped inside. A sickly decaying smell assaulted his nose as he walked through. The stench was overpowering. Fog rolled thick and heavy around his legs as he walked further into the room. The floor beneath the fog was squishy and full of mud. Indy looked around the room and realized he couldn't see any walls. Even behind him, only the fog swirled in his wake, the door had disappeared.

As he walked on in confusion, Indy started stumbling on things hidden in the mud and water at his feet. The muddy water continued to get deeper and the room, if you still consider it a room, seemed to get darker. Sounds floated in the fog as he walked on. Birds, crickets, and frogs sang in the low light. Occasionally he heard something larger splashing through the water but nothing was visible in the mist. A forest of broken black decaying trees rose up ahead of him from the dark water. Several trunks loomed high above him, their dark rotted corpse's just shells of their former glory. There was debris and other garbage in the water floating by as he slogged on. Indy felt dizzy as he marched through the decaying waste.

He couldn't understand how he hadn't reached the other side of the tower room by now. He didn't know where he was going or even what he was supposed to do. The apple he had eaten was really doing a number on his senses right now.

The fog in front on him started to brighten and there was a shaft of sunlight not far off. Seeing nothing else of interest Indy started off in the direction of the sunlight.

As he got closer to the light, the fog seemed to melt away. In its place, the light illuminated a small island of green grass and a large pile of garbage. Tiny white branches poked out from under the trash like infant arms reaching out for their mother.

Indy climbed from the dirty water and sat on the green grass regarding the pale white limbs. He started to pull the trash from around a small white seedling. Carefully he stripped the small tree of the clutter. When the tree was finally clear of the garbage, it seemed much bigger. In fact, he was sure that a moment ago the tree was nothing but a seedling. Now clear of the debris he thought the tree at least a yearling.

Indy looked up at the spot of sunlight high overhead. It looked like it was shining through a large hole in the ceiling. If he wasn't mistaken, he could just make out the Eden tree symbol around the lip of the hole. Looking back and forth from the fast growing white tree to the ceiling Indy began to get an idea of his challenge.

He needed to grow the tree tall enough to climb up through the hole. Indy cleared more debris from the tree and piled it high on one corner of the island. He dug at rocks clogging the tree roots around the tree and piled them atop the trash. Several items he found in the garbage proved to be useful. He poked a large metal bucket full of holes with a broken screwdriver. He used the bucket as a crude filter to fetch dirty, muddy water for the tree. As he continued to work, the tree responded and grew.

The light from the ceiling seemed to brighten as well and soon the tree was tall enough to poke through the ceiling above.

Indy hated heights but he knew he needed to hurry up his pace so he grabbed onto the tree and started to climb. The tree had so many handholds it was like climbing a very sturdy ladder and in moments, he was up and through the hole.

The tree continued to grow as he stepped from the branches. In fact, by the time he had stepped off the tree its trunk had filled the hole completely.

"No going back I guess," Indy said as he looked down at the thick trunk of tree and then around for his next test. He was in a large stone room that seemed to be a shrine to the white tree that was standing tall behind him. A door stood at the far end of the room that was decorated with another symbol he recognized from Eden's tower walls. The symbol was of two crossed swords atop a blue circle, it was Valhalla.

EDEN 26 - VALHALLA

The stone and wood room he stepped into was filled with large angry men. Some of them wore heavy metal armour and some wore hardly anything at all. The mass of men were busy throwing themselves up a small hill at the center of the room. Atop the hill was a monster that stood tall above them all. This creature absolutely towered over them. It was almost ten feet tall with pale blue skin and flaming red hair. Large bony tusks protruded from its lips and head. The monster had a heavily muscled frame and huge three fingered hands. It wore nothing save for a red and black leather kilt wrapped around its waist.

Indy could see something glinting around its thick neck in the hazy light. It looked like a small golden key hung from a tight golden necklace at the base of its throat.

Indy looked past the creature and closer at the room around him. There on the far side of the room was another large wooden door. He could see metal embossed on the door forming two crossed swords. Below the crossed swords, Indy could see a golden keyhole.

There was the challenge. "Ok… so get the key, open the lock. That seems easy enough," he said to himself.

Just then a heavily armoured man thudded to the ground at his feet. The man cursed and swore before rising to his feet and dashing back towards the hill. Indy watched the man run at the monster only to be launched in another direction by a sweeping kick.

Indy realized the beast was just toying with these people. The beast was sweeping them off the hill by the dozen with a single heavy blow. Indy watched in fascination as a warrior tried to sneak up on the creature, low and from behind. The beast picked that one up with a three-toed foot. The large blue foot pawed the earth and the man was thrown away like a ragdoll.

The man sailed through the air and crumpled against the wall. This time he didn't rise like the others.

No one came to the fallen warrior's aid. The others continued to assault the hill in one mindless wave. Indy raced over to the man, who was struggling to his feet.

Indy reached down to help pull the man up to his feet. Indy looked into a single shocked blue eye as the man rose to tower over him. Long blonde hair and a longer beard covered the man's face. A giant scar cut across the left side of his face and through his left eye socket. He had a large red ruby in place of the missing eye. The man's other eye looked at him wearily.

"Just who are ya now?" The warrior demanded.

"My name is Indy," Indy replied with his usual grin.

"Ye risk Odin's wrath to aid me, Indy. But thank ye kindly. I'm Gammon Windsong." Gammon bowed low but stood quickly. "I must re-join the fight." Gammon moved to leave but stilled when Indy raised a hand.

"Well," he said impatiently. "What is it?"

"What is that monster?" Indy asked. "And where am I?"

Gammon raised one thick eyebrow in surprise. "You're in the halls of the brave in the castle of Odin and that beast there is a berserker. We are in training for Ragnarok. Anyone that defeats the berserkers may sup with Odin and the other gods. Didn't the Valkyries tell you all this when they dropped you on the tower?"

"No," Indy replied. "I came up a white tree, I didn't see any Valkyries."

"Odin preserve us," Gammon swore. "You climbed Yggdrasil, the great tree of life? You are a braver man than I. But why did you risk your life to come here."

"I am trying to save the tower of Eden. That berserker there holds a key," Indy said as he pointed to the monster. "I need that key to continue on my fight to save my people and if I fail, all my friends will die."

"A noble quest it is," Gammon said.

"I need your help, I don't think I can do this alone. Will you help me?" Indy asked, pointing at the mob of men surrounding the monster.

"Aye Indy, I will help you." Gammon took a hunters horn from his thick leather belt and blew two shrill notes. The men in the chamber paused their assault to look their way.

Gammon bellowed at his fellow warriors. "The champion of Eden and climber of Yggdrasil asks a boon of this great hall. His quest takes him from this hall through the locked portal of Valhalla. As you all know, the berserker holds the only known key. My friend here requests passage to the great beast. Shall we aid our fellow warrior in his time of need?"

"Aye!" The warriors shouted and parted to make a wide path leading to the hill.

Gammon walked the path of warriors at Indy's shoulder. Men bowed their heads in respect as they both passed. In

217

seconds, they stood at the base of the hill looking up at the blue-skinned berserker. Behind him, the rows of warriors formed a ring around them. Gammon slapped his shoulder with a heavy hand as the warrior nodded and stepped away.

The berserker leaned down to glare at Indy with a pair of dark hostile eyes. Its breath blew into Indy's face as the beast huffed its obvious disapproval of him. Its breath smelled of rotting flesh and sour wine. The beast stood up to its full height and bellowed a challenge at him. Indy prepared to move but something was nagging him at the back of his mind. Instead, he started to circle the base of the hill, trying to buy his brain time to think.

Indy worked his shoulders trying to loosen them up when it finally dawned on him what was wrong. Gammons slap had stung. It was a small pain but… the dragon tattoo was not protecting him. The realization came too late. Large three fingered hands reached down from above to grab him. Air rushed by his face as the berserker lifted him high over its head.

Indy looked down on the berserker's fiery red hair and down further to the giant warriors surrounding the base of the hill. A hush filled the room as Indy looked down among the warriors. He found Gammon's one eye looking back up at him. Gammon smiled and nodded at Indy. His one good eye winked.

Hope flooded Indy as Gammon raised a hand and dropped it. The berserkers grip relaxed slightly as it realized what was about to happen.

"Charge!" Shouted Gammon.

The ring of warriors around the hill flooded forward. Indy reached down the berserkers face to grab hold of one of its long tusks. With a tremendous heave, Indy pulled it, as the berserker started to kick at the rushing warriors. Several men had grabbed hold of the beast's giant legs and tried to bring it down. The berserker released its hold on Indy as it tried to swat the warriors off its legs. Indy was left to dangle from one long tusk. For a moment, the key was at his eye level. A furious shake of the berserkers head caused Indy to slip and almost let go of his hold.

Indy struggled to maintain his grip as he was flung back and forth. For an instant, the beast's head stopped moving and the key swung around its neck in front of him. Seizing the chance Indy grabbed for the key with both hands.

Indy landed heavily on the hill but didn't have time to stop and catch his breath. A three-toed foot stomped down and kicked him backwards through the press of bodies. He soared over their heads and landed hard against the stone wall. Indy lay there panting and out of breath. Pain flooded through his right arm and shoulder from smashing into the wall. A dark shadow suddenly blocked the light from the room and rough hands seized him and lifted him back onto his feet.

"Well done, well done indeed," Gammon said. "We almost had him that time."

Indy held up one fist. When he opened his hand, a small gold key lay on his palm.

Gammon gave a little bow. "A fine fought battle my friend. But my battle still rages on. Until we meet again. Good luck." The warrior turned and sprinted back to the hill.

Indy turned from the lopsided battle to regard the door that was decorated with a silver circle and crossed with two swords.

The small keyhole accepted the gold key and turned with a soft click. Indy left the battle raging behind him and stepped through the door.

EDEN 27 - HADES

A short flight of stone stairs rose up along the towers curved wall. Candles flickered in sconces along the wall lighting his path in a dull warm glow.

At the top of the stairs, there was yet another door. The symbol on this one showed a burned and cracked planet, surrounded by a glowing blue circle. Something about the symbol raised goosebumps on his flesh. If he remembered right, it was the symbol for Hades.

The door swung open at his touch. Beyond it laid a burned and broken... shopping mall. The mall spread out in front of him with closed and barred shops on either side of a long hallway. At the far end of the mall, behind several glass doors, he saw a shimmering aurora.

Figures moved around on the other side of the aurora but he couldn't see much from this distance. Indy headed for the shimmering lights at a quick pace. Without warning, a small dog darted at him from out of sight and nipped him on the leg. The dog's sharp little teeth dug into his leg just above his ankle. Indy cursed at the dog as it ran away to whatever hole it came from. Indy watched as the little dog ducked under a metal gate fronting a sporting goods store. At the back of the store, Indy caught a glimpse of a black swirling vortex that flickered with small bursts of lightning. The vortex throbbed

221

with a dark hungry power Indy could feel in his bones. He had taken several steps toward the store without realizing it. When Indy walked head first into the half-closed security gate, he stopped. Adams warning came back to him then.

The black vortex seemed to fade a bit as he watched but he was distracted from its hypnotic motion when his ankle started to throb with pain. Indy knelt to check the wound and saw little droplets of blood seeping through his sock.

More growling came behind him as a large pack of dogs came around the far corner of the mall. These dogs were all in rough shape. Each dog was lean to the point individual ribs were clearly visible. The thick black hair covering their bodies was matted in spots and dark patches of skin hung like flaps from their legs. As he watched, each dog fixed him with a burning red gaze. Thick black smoke puffed out from their mouths as they stared at him. Indy turned and ran for the far doors and the aurora beyond.

The pack of dogs growled and took up chase. Only a pair of double doors blocked Indy's path to the aurora. The first of the doors opened with a quick tug and closed behind him just as a dog rammed into it with a thud. The dog snarled and bit at the glass but wasn't able to break through. Indy yanked on the next set of doors but they were barred shut.

He banged on the door. "Let me in," he screamed. The aurora shimmered just on the other side of the glass and three people came running to his shouts. Each of them wore a long black coat and high leather boots. The clothes he could see under the cloaks were also a thick black leather.

"A survivor!" the first one to the door called.

"Get him inside," the second black cloak cried.

"Wait, remember the rules." cautioned the third.

The three in black each wore a thick metal grill over their mouths, hiding most of their face. They also wore dark sunglasses that hid their eyes and gave them a dark sinister look. The glasses shifted up and down as they looked over Indy and his clothes.

"Have you been bitten?" asked the first in a stern but hushed voice.

"You can't come in if you have been bitten," said the second.

"You'll kill us all if you are infected." warned the third.

All of the dogs had reached the doors now. Each snarled and threw itself at the glass doors. Already the glass was fracturing and little black smoke clouds seeped through.

Their words gave him pause, time to think in the chaos of the moment. Indy thought he was going to die if he didn't get through those doors. But what about those people inside, if he really were infected, he could bring death among them. Others had grouped up behind the three upon hearing the disruption. Men, women, and children stood watching him, waiting for his answer. He couldn't take the risk. He didn't know if he was infected but it was something he couldn't take a chance on.

"A small dog bit me just a few minutes ago," he said in a whisper.

The crowd gasped and some cried in horror.

The three in black nodded their heads in understanding.

Several bloody black muzzles were through the glass now and Indy's shoulders slumped. He was out of time and options.

"We know," said one.

"We saw," said the second.

"You must flee," said the third.

They all pointed to a fire exit between the two sets of doors just feet from him. Indy didn't recall seeing the door before but he didn't hesitate.

Indy ran for the fire exit door and not a moment too soon. Glass shattered behind him as the dogs broke through. He ran at the fire exit and shoulder charged his way through. Spinning quickly he slammed the door shut behind him.

EDEN 28 - OLYMPUS

Indy stood panting with his eyes shut and hands bracing against the door. When no sounds came from the other side of the door, he raised his head and opened his eyes. Two lightning bolts spearing a large circle were carved into the back of the door. He must have passed the last test, although he wasn't quite sure what the test had been. He did however recognize the lightning bolt symbol for Olympus.

Indy stood tall and looked at his surroundings. The door he had passed through was part of a large broken tower. Blocks of stone littered the ground all the way to the edge of the rocks. The tower stood on a large outcropping of rocks surrounded by the swell of an enormous ocean. An earthquake or landslide must have caused part of the stone tower to collapse and slide into the water. Only the door and a small portion of the stone wall remained.

There was nothing else on the small little Island. But Indy could hear a soft wooden banging from down near the water. Indy looked over the edge and spotted a small boat drifting in the water at the base of the rock island. It was moored to the rocks by a frayed and knotted piece of rope. The boat had a name "Penny" painted in blue on the back of its wooden frame.

Looking past the small bobbing boat, Indy regarded the water. For as far as he could see there was only crashing waves. The sky above was dark, ominous, and lightning danced among the dark black clouds. Thunder boomed and the wind started to pick up. The wind was so strong it threatened to lift Indy off his feet. The little boat started to pull free from its knotted anchor and Indy had to run as the boat started out to sea. He landed in the small boat hard and his weight alone threatened to sink the small craft. Splashing water rose up several times to pour into the boat. The boat started to spin in circles as it caught the current and drifted out to sea.

The wind blew and water crashed for an eternity before something new broke the scenery. The boat was heading for another small rocky island, just barely bigger than the one he just left. This one was different in another way as well. Two people clung to each other atop the rocks and waved wildly at Indy once they spotted him. The small boat was drifting by when one of the people on the rocks threw out a tough soggy rope. Indy caught the rope and tied it to the boat.

The man standing at the far end of the rope pulled the small boat to shore with a mighty effort. A smaller woman stood beside the man, cheering him on. Once Penny's boat got close enough, the woman ran to the edge of the rocks and helped Indy guide the boat in.

"Thank heavens you came." the woman cried. "We have been stuck on this rock for days."

The man ran up behind her and held out his hand. "I'm Dean Jones and this is my wife Martha."

Indy shook the man's hand.

Martha spoke up quickly after looking up at the dark sky. "We need to go soon Dean. The storm is about to break and you remember what it did to the last boat."

"Yes, I remember Martha, you haven't stopped reminding me of it for days now." Dean said with a great huff. "Your boat is a little small stranger, but Port Haven is not far away. Can we share your boat until then?"

Indy nodded and helped Martha into the boat. There was barely enough room for the woman to sit and the waves started to lap at the rails.

Dean frowned at the boat and shook his head sadly. "That won't do, not at all," he said. "The boat just isn't big enough for all three of us. Please, just take my wife into Port Haven and have them send out a bigger boat for me. I will wait here," The man crossed his arms stubbornly and nodded at Indy.

"I don't know how to get there. I don't even know where I am," Indy said. In a quieter voice, he added. "Or even what I'm supposed to do."

Indy looked around the island for a clue or one of the symbols but there was nothing to guide his way.

He looked at Martha and her husband as they stared at each other with desperation clearly visible on their faces. It tore at Indy's heart and there was no way he was going to separate the two of them.

"Since you know the way, why don't you take the boat Dean? You can send someone back for me."

Relief washed over Martha's face as Dean considered the offer. "I can't begin to thank you enough…"

"Call me Indy. Just take care of your wife, Dean. I'll be okay," Indy's words were lost as the lightning and thunder shook the rocks around them. The waves started to pound the little boat relentlessly. If they didn't get going soon, the little boat would be smashed upon the rocks.

Indy leapt from the boat as Dean took his place.

The boat dipped slightly deeper in the water as they switched places but stayed afloat.

Indy grabbed up Dean's backpack and moved to hand it to him.

"Keep it with my blessing. You may need what few supplies it holds." Dean gave a slight bow of his head and pushed off from the rocks.

"Thank you and god bless." Martha shouted as the boat drifted away. She was still waving as the boat disappeared in the distance.

Indy hefted the backpack on his shoulder and began to scout the island. It didn't take long and when he was done, he sat down at the center of the small rock island to consider his options. Something inside the backpack clinked as he set it down. He ignored it as the sun started to break through the clouds. Bright light warmed his face as the sun's rays covered the island in a soft warm glow.

Indy looked into the clearing sky and saw the sunrays coming through… a hole in the ceiling. He stood quickly and strained his neck for a better look. Small symbols dotted the area around the hole. The twin lightning bolts that made up the Olympus symbol ran around the outer edge of the hole. Indy wished he had kept the boats mooring rope but a second look at the hole told him it would have come up way short anyhow.

Indy bumped the backpack with his foot and heard the muffled clink again. Out of curiosity, he opened the bag. He pulled out two oblong black discs. Each disc had a raised edge and a thick blue gel coating the inside. The gel reminded him of the sticky surface on the AGPs. Indy studied the two shapes a little longer before a thought came to him. He put the two discs on the ground and slipped his feet into them. When he put his feet into the gel, he felt a slight jolt of energy run up his legs and a familiar sticky sensation.

Thrump thrump thrumpt.

The discs hesitated a moment before lifting free from the ground and it took a few more minutes before Indy found his balance. Indy hovered in the air a moment longer before stretching his toes out. When that didn't work, he tried jumping. The discs responded by rising slowly up into the air. When Indy tried to crouch down to check his footing, the discs started to descend.

"Geez, seems like I can't get enough of heights lately. Why does it always have to be heights," Indy closed his eyes and concentrated on not thinking about heights. With his eyes closed, he started to hop. Within a few minutes, his head bumped softly on the stone ceiling high above. He was only a few feet from the hole he had spotted from the ground. Using his hands Indy clawed at the rough stone ceiling and made his way over and then up into the hole.

EDEN 29 - ATLANTIS

He passed through the hole in a blink and then Indy was in a new chamber. This one was almost exactly the same as Adams room downstairs. Tapestries hung the walls and bookshelves and desks cluttered the room. There was one major difference however. In the center of this room, there was a lazy boy recliner. Below the recliner, Indy could see a large symbol etched into the floor. This symbol only showed a blue circle that contained a large black square that was open on one end. It was the towers symbol for Atlantis.

A box matching the one in the symbol sat in one corner of the room. Indy walked over to the box and lifted the lid. Inside the black box, there was a toolbox and a spider-like winged creature. Indy reached in to touch the unmoving spider thing. It was made of a hard cold metal. The thin crystal wings of the creature turned blue at his touch. A tiny thrump thrump thrumpt started coming from it as it rose from the box. The flying spider hovered around his head as Indy pulled the toolbox out to inspect it. Inside the toolbox, he found basic tools, a sledgehammer, a regular hammer, some nails, a saw, and a length of rope. Indy looked around for a clue on how to proceed. Not finding anything interesting at first glance, he left the toolbox on the ground and walked over to inspect the chair in the center of the room. The chair was made of a soft white material that was heavily cushioned. Feeling a bit weary, Indy sat down in the chair and reclined his feet up to relax a moment. A dull humming vibrated from the chair.

"Ahhh that's pretty comfy," Indy said as he relaxed into the soft warm cushions. "I could go for a pillow though." The spider fly buzzed around the room and picked up a cushion from a chair near the wall. The small fly struggled to bring him the pillow and after a full minute of effort, was finally able to drop it in his lap.

"Thank you," Indy told it. "Too bad you weren't a bit bigger, you could have brought that a little easier."

The black box in the corner hummed and then out came another spider fly. This one was a bit bigger than the first.

"That's incredible!" Indy yelled. The box made him another spider fly robot thing to do his bidding. He had to test it out. "Ok, spiderbots bring me another pillow," he commanded.

Both spiderbots obeyed instantly. The pair of them buzzed around the room until they found another pillow. Together they worked to bring him the pillow.

I wonder what else that box can make. He thought as he lay atop his pillows.

Another spiderbot popped out of the box and flew over to the others hovering near Indy.

"Hmmm," Indy said. "Thought controlled."

"Find me a way to the roof of this tower," he commanded.

The little robots flew around the room for a few minutes before landing on the far wall. With a small effort, Indy rose from the deep cushions and pillows. Indy walked over to the spiderbots and saw they were clustered around a small square hole in the wall.

"Out of the way, move it," he said brushing one of the spiderbots away. The bot chirped at him and moved back to the hole. Indy was able to make out a large wooden door on the other side of the wall before the bot obstructed his view.

"Make the hole bigger," he told the spiderbots.

Not a single robot moved.

Indy slapped his head in instant realization. They listen to the chair.

He dashed back over to the chair and hopped in. He reissued his last command to widen the hole. All three spiderbots started to chip away slowly at the hole. Small bits of stone dropped to the floor as they worked. Indy realized quickly that way would take days.

Maybe the box could make me something better suited to digging through stone.

He issued an order to the black box, "Create a new creature that can tunnel through rock."

The box hummed and a new spider type creature popped out onto the floor. This one was smaller than the others and had no wings. It crawled over to him, awaiting a command.

"Make me a hole through that wall," he said.

The little bot scurried over to the wall and started to burrow through it at floor level. A few seconds later, it returned to the chair.

"No, no, no, I need a hole I can get through. Make the hole bigger." The spiderbot hustled to obey making another small hole beside the first. This time it didn't stop after it made the hole. It continued to make random holes, all at floor level.

It was time to make another command decision. Indy called to the box to make him one hundred of those creatures.

The box shook violently and out popped a swarm of one hundred small spiderbots with wings. They were quickly followed by one hundred slightly larger spiderbots and then one hundred crawling spiderbots. They all swarmed over to the control chair.

Indy's patience was wearing thin and his frustration leaked into his next commands.

"Tear that wall down and get me to the other side," he demanded of the spiderbot creatures.

The bots obeyed. They attacked the wall viciously. Several were damaged in the first few seconds and fluttered to the floor, useless.

So he ordered the box to build him a creature to fix the others.

A red and white spiderbot popped out of the box with wings larger than the rest. It went around the room collecting fallen workers and dropping them into the box. Seconds later a refurbished bug bot would pop out and go back to work. Satisfied, Indy leaned back and made himself comfortable. The day had worn on him and the comfy chair lulled him to sleep.

Crash!

Indy's eyes popped open when a large section of the wall crashed into the floor. Indy looked out of the large hole to a spectacular view. It looked like he was high above a lush tropical island dotted with white sandy beaches and wooden huts.

But there was a problem, the damn spiderbots had brought down the wrong wall. When he looked around the room at the destruction the little bots caused, he realized the truth. They had done exactly what he had told them to do. In his haste to get through the wall, Indy had forgotten one important detail. In a circular room, there was only one wall.

The bots stopped their work at that moment and came swarming over him. Confused, Indy did not know what was happening until it was too late. The spiderbots dragged Indy from the chair and towards the opening in the tower wall. The little bots were dragging, pushing, or pulling as hard as they could. Indy flailed his arms and legs but whenever one bot fell away there was another there to take its place.

The edge of the tower grew closer and his vertigo picked that moment to kick in. Indy stopped fighting the bots as he grew dizzy and light headed. A section of the wall scraped against his back and arm as he was dragged out of the room. The world below him fell away as the bots released their grip and returned inside the room without him.

Indy was left hanging by one arm as the crumbling wall continued to give way. As the last bot flew away, he lifted himself back into the room. All of the little bots had gone dormant and were sitting quietly on the cushioned white chair.

The spiderbots didn't begin to move again until he was all the way back across the broken wall and into the room. Several lifted away from the cushions and hovered over the chair, possibly prepared to continue with their orders to place him outside the wall. Indy held his breath for a minute but when the bots didn't come any closer, he relaxed. Making his way carefully around the outer edge of the room, he found that the way to the next door had been cleared for him. In fact, the wall he wanted to get through looked like a giant piece of Swiss cheese. Indy picked the closest hole and crawled through.

Looking back over his shoulder Indy noticed the tools scattered around the toolbox. How much easier would it have been just to break down the wall by himself? Indy shrugged and looked at the next door.

The wooden door stood large and imposing. It was by far the biggest of the doors he had come across so far. The symbol on this door activated when he pressed his hands to the wood of the door. A blue circle flared to life quickly followed by a splash of blue forming a familiar shape... a dragon. This had to be it, the control room. Indy took a deep breath and pushed into the room.

EDEN 30 – DRAGONS DEN

When Indy stepped into the room, the first thing he saw was Zeus. The large man was still wearing his black military fatigues and boots. A tattered black cloak enveloped his large squared shoulders. The man's eyes seemed to burn with a hatred Indy couldn't even begin to understand.

"Ahh, Mr. Locke. I am so glad that you could join me, this fine day. I hope you've had a pleasant journey?"

Zeus grunted and walked over to a white and black box at the center of the room. Indy looked a little closer at the box and noticed it wasn't the box that was black, but the thick tangle of vines wrapped around it. The blue light that pulsed from the vines seemed darker than before... and it reminded him of leeches instead of vines. Zeus was standing over the box smiling down on it. His big hands reached down and lifted open the lid. Zeus reached into the box and came out with a large black artifact. It was a long stick as thick as his thumb and wrapped with a thick thorny rope. At one end of the rope, a pair of black wings spread out to either side. Between the wings, a small diamond shaped head sat staring his way. The head looked very familiar. An electric tingle spread down from his chest to his wrist. Indy glanced down to look at his wrist. A matching black head looked back at him. Relief flooded through him as Indy realized his power had returned. It also suddenly dawned on him he knew what Zeus was holding. It was a real dragon.

Zeus held up the rod and poked the little dragon with his finger. The dragon hissed and spit but finally let go of the rod. Black wings snapped out as the thing fell. With a rush of wings, the dragon flew by Indy and landed easily on a bookcase behind him. Other dark shapes poked their heads from darken corners as Indy watched.

Zeus threw the now empty rod to a far corner and the rod clanged against a dozen other similar forms already on the floor.

"Bah, useless little snakes!" Zeus roared. "The box won't make anything but those blasted creatures now."

Zeus turned his evil glare on Indy. "So what do you want Locke? Come to torment me a little more, in this prison of mine?"

Indy stood tall, determined not to show Zeus a lick of fear or respect. "Whatever you have done to the tower is threatening the valley. Everything my mom worked so hard to do is going to be destroyed. All the people in this valley will die Zeus. Adam is going to shut off the tower unless I can fix things in here."

"Ha-ha you're going to fix things? You're gonna fix things? Tell me Daniel Locke, junior, how are you going to fix this."

The tattered black cloak on Zeus's shoulders twitched and then unfurled like two sails. Long black wings expanded to almost the width of the room. Zeus's eyes began to burn with a red fire and the evil glare darkened.

"Tell me again how you are going to fix... things. This is my tower now. The valley outside these walls will be mine...

Hell the world too while I am at it. Nothing will stand against the power I now possess," Zeus held his arms above his head and black lightning arced across every inch of his massive body. "You will be the first of my many slaves little Daniel Locke. Bow down before me and I shall spare your friends. Bow down before your new GOD!

Zeus cackled madly as his tattered black wings beat a strong rhythm in time to his laughs. The dragons around the outside of the room began to hiss and spit at the disturbing noise.

Indy stood in shock as Zeus came at him. The man had been quick before, even for his size. Now the man blurred when he moved. Black gloved hands grabbed Indy and threw him to the floor. Heavy combat boots stomped all over his body and kicked at his ribs. The kicks didn't hurt but the strength behind them knocked Indy dizzy. Again, Zeus grabbed him, this time by the throat. Indy was lifted high into the air and thrown into the far corner. A burst of black lightning followed him into the corner and coursed over Indy without any noticeable effect. Zeus stared down on him with an evil glare, obviously bothered by the lack of response to the powerful lightning attack.

Zeus turned his back on Indy and strode to a large tapestry hanging on the wall. In one quick movement, he tore the hanging from the wall. It revealed a large arched window. Outside the window, they could see the castle and giant white tree on the coast. A full moon had risen over the water and lit the scene from above.

Zeus was stretching his wings wide with his hands pressed up against the window. "Once I break free from this prison, I will fly from this tower and seize your pitiful castle for myself. Nothing will stand in my way. Anyone who does…" Zeus smiled wickedly.

Indy thought he could see pointed teeth in the man's smile. A chill rushed down his spine at the thought of this monster leaving the tower. His stomach heaved when he remembered Adams warning, that the evil would threaten the whole planet. This was the reason he was here. Zeus was the corruption that had to be removed. Indy tried to stand but slipped over something on the floor. A long rod rolled away from his foot and crashed into a pile of other rods. Now that he was closer, Indy recognized the rods for what they really were.

They were dragon sticks. Indy dove into the pile and wrapped his hands around two of them. When he stood from the pile, on instinct, he raised the sticks and tapped them together twice. Blue light flared around the sticks and that caused Zeus to pause a moment. The large man regarded Indy quietly and then gazed longingly at the dragon sticks in his hands.

Indy went on the attack. The sticks were spinning in his hands and buzzing through the air. The first one hit Zeus hard on the left arm. The second came in low and tagged Zeus on his hip. Both hits caused the big man to fall back in pain.

Zeus wasn't dumb, he instantly recognized the danger the sticks posed to him. In a flash, one of his wings swept out to brush Indy aside and Zeus raced to grab a pair of the dragon sticks for himself. Zeus tapped the pair of sticks together and they flared blue with small flashes of black lightning tracing their length.

239

When the two fighters came together in the center of the room Indy knew right away that he was outmatched. Zeus was bigger, faster, and stronger. He also knew a lot more about fighting. Buzzing sticks flared and flashed as Indy was hit by several strong blows.

One smashed him hard in the stomach and he fell to his knees. Zeus followed up the blow with a strong kick to the head, sending Indy skidding back to the center of the room. Indy crashed into the box and sat dazed for a second trying to steady himself. A blue and black vine pulsed only inches from his face. The vine was pulsing like a heart. He could even feel its rhythm vibrating deep within his chest.

Indy reached out to the vine and slipped a hand around one thick branch. A buzzing filled his ears and thoughts and the world around him seemed to darken for a second or two. The heat of the dragon tattoo faded and he was left shivering and cold. Indy could feel all his strength and energy draining from his body in a rush as he held onto the black vine. Indy knew Zeus was coming for him but he was mesmerized by the colors swirling through his mind. Only the thump of a dragon stick crashing down on his spine brought him out of the daze. Pain filled his head and he screamed a loud piercing cry. The hand that was gripping the vine seized up involuntarily. The vine tore away from the box as Indy curled up into a ball, hand still wrapped tightly around the vine.

Zeus fell to one knee at the same time. Horror filled his eyes and the black wings at his back seemed to droop. They both looked at the box and vines that were gushing jets of a tarry black liquid. Indy could barely see through the haze of pain in his head but he realized this was his only chance. The black vines were the source of Zeus's power. Indy crawled slowly back to the box and grabbed at several more vines. He was ready to pull when a hand wrapped around his ankle.

Indy looked back to see Zeus with a pleading look on his face. "Please Indy," he said. "Don't do it. That box drove me mad, I couldn't help it."

When Indy didn't release his hold on the vines, anger filled Zeus's fiery red eyes. "James was right about you from the beginning," Zeus said through an angry sneer. "He called you trouble and a pain. But he also told me a little secret about you. I know something about you that your father has kept from you for years. Something I will tell you, if you let go of those vines."

Indy considered the offer only a second before he spoke. "Whatever you could tell me doesn't matter. James is dead. I killed him two weeks ago on the beach. Either way, whatever you could tell me isn't worth the lives of my friends."

Indy tugged hard on the vines as he felt Zeus start climbing his leg hand over hand. Trickles of black lightning began to arc across his legs but there was little power behind them. The vines in his hands wouldn't give and Indy kept tugging on them in desperation. Several vines ripped away from the box as Zeus put his hands around Indy's throat. Black liquid splashed over them both as Indy gave one final heave. The last of the blackened vines fell away from the white box and Zeus rolled off Indy's body in a dead heap.

Indy watched in horror as Zeus's body started to shake, black crystals beginning to form on the big black wings. The black crystals started to spread over the man's entire body as Indy watched. The body stopped shaking for a moment and Indy thought it was all over. Just as he took a long deep breath and relaxed, Zeus's head snapped around and stared directly at Indy. In a reflex motion, Indy scooped up a nearby dragon stick and brought it down on Zeus head. Black dust exploded around him as the blackened body disintegrated.

EDEN 31 – QUESTIONS AND ANSWERS

As the dust around him settled, a light flashed somewhere above, near the white box. Indy stood slowly and found Adam sitting atop the box smiling at him. The room around him had changed as well. Six large circular windows now dotted the wall. There was even a large archway leading to a balcony where the large glass window had stood only moments before.

"You have done it Indy, the tower is cleansed," Adam said. "With any luck by the time you get back to the castle you will have a surprise waiting for you."

"That's it?" Indy asked. "No thank you or words of wisdom? I could use at least a couple of questions answered after getting my butt handed to me."

Adam looked thoughtfully at him and nodded his head. "Yes, I do think you deserve a few answers. Go ahead, you should have enough time to ask a few quick questions. I will try to answer what I can, Guardian."

In the distance, Indy heard a deep rumbling noise.

Adam lifted his head and cocked an ear at the noise. We are running very short of time. This tower must be hidden away where it will be safe.

Indy pondered a moment before rattling off the first questions that came to his mind. "Is my mom still alive?" he asked.

"Yes," Adam said. "However your mom's body and soul is entwined in the great white tree. She lives as long as the tree lives."

Indy smiled at that small bit of hope and asked his next question. "Who built the tower?"

"I did," Adams chest swelled with pride. "Six meteors shot to earth millions of years ago. Each contained a small white box. Each box contains an artificial intelligence dedicated to building and maintaining a specific tower design. Each tower has a specific purpose meant to safeguard humanity in the most extreme situations."

Indy was shocked by that one. He looked in awe at the small man sitting atop the box.

"Your next question? Adam prompted as Indy stared at him."

Most of the other questions Indy had planned slipped from his mind. He noticed his dragon tattoo swirling on the back of his hand. Another question came to mind. "Is James alive?"

"Yes, James survived your beach encounter and has found and entered the tower of Valhalla."

Indy grunted with displeasure at that bit of news.

"What about Zeus, why was he... changed?"

Adam was silent for a time and Indy wasn't sure the small man would answer. A small tear trickled down Adams face. "There are many safeguards put in place on this tower but there is one thing that I cannot prevent. In the end, I cannot save a person who does not want to be saved. Zeus's greed corrupted his wish and created the monster you saw here. The only way I could safe guard the people of this valley was to imprison him where he could do no harm."

Adam looked down at the black dust coating the floor and shook his head again. "Unfortunately, the man was able to infect the control box with his greed. The energy the tower was forced to expend to contain him was quite high. Under normal circumstances, only a guardian has access to this room. While Zeus was imprisoned, he was allowed unlimited access to the control box. Although I enacted a controlled loop so that his access was severely restricted. I could not foresee the man's wanton desire corrupting the very source of this tower's power. He was still given each of his wishes although he didn't realize all that he asked for was given."

"What about this tower? How long will the aurora last now that Zeus is gone?"

"I will maintain the aurora for as long as the need for it exists. A good guess would be about six years. In order to heal the earth to a level that can be properly maintained, it will take at least that long if not longer."

Indy nodded slowly, happy that they would be safe for the time being. "You said James was still alive and inside the tower of Valhalla. Where's the other tower?"

Adam looked around the room, seeming to stare out each of the six windows around the room before he said. "Currently the other Valhalla is floating high over the Hawaiian islands. It looks to be on a direct course for this tower." The window Adam was looking at had swirled and shifted to a different view. A large chunk of land was drifting in fluffy white clouds high over a group of islands.

The news brought a flutter of panic to Indy's heart. James was a traitor and had threatened his father's life. It wasn't hard to guess his motives, after everything that had happened. James wanted power and he would not stop at anything to get it.

The room shook around him and several books fell from the shelves. A few of the small black dragons hiding in the shadows were startled into flight. They flapped around the room and buzzed around their heads.

"You are running out of time my friend," Adam said with a small smile. "You may ask one last question before you must go."

"Who or what are you?" Indy asked as several dragons settled on the little man's shoulders.

Adam smiled and his eyes lit with a soft blue light. "I am a construct of the control box," he patted the white box he sat on. "My main task is as an interface to communicate with intelligence races, such as you."

The room started to shake as the rumbling grew even louder. Adam slid off the white box causing the dragons perched on his shoulders to fly off. Adam took Indy by the hand and walked him to the archway leading to a small balcony. The valley around them surged and shifted in the distance. With sudden realization Indy realized it wasn't the scenery shifting it was the tower. The tower was sinking fast into the ground.

"Take care Indy, I will see you again," Adam said. The little man smiled as he pushed Indy over the balcony rail. Indy fell... a few feet before landing on the valley ground. The tower continued to slide past him as he watched. In a few moments the ground had swallowed the tower whole. The rumbling continued as the dirt caved in around where the tower had been just moments ago.

Within minutes, all that was left of the tower was a deep depression of freshly turned earth. A small puddle of water started to form in the bottom of the depression. Indy didn't know if it was a trick of the moonlight but the water down there appeared almost silver.

Indy stood and brushed his clothes off.

He watched the silvery water filling the depression for a moment, wishing he had had more time to talk to Adam. Indy sighed and turned around, heading back to the castle, eager to bring news of his victory back to his friends. He also had a warning to deliver to his father. James was still alive and Valhalla was coming.

THE END

10616123R00159

Made in the USA
Charleston, SC
18 December 2011